Sightline
By
T.M. Erwin

SIGHTLINE

First edition. February 14, 2022.

Copyright © 2022 T.M. Erwin.

ISBN: 979-8201162597

Written by T.M. Erwin.

Thanks to my wife Ann for her understanding,.

and to

Kelly Francis for her invaluable help

Sightline
Prologue

Approximately 1000 ad
L'Anse aux Meadows
Northern tip of what is now Newfoundland, Canada.

THE WEATHER-BEATEN Viking long ship was pulled up and anchored on the beach, as some of the crew unloaded supplies onto the rocky shore and others prepared to set up camp for the night. Everybody on the crew knew their job to do and performed it efficiently. The leader of the group was a six- foot tall, blonde, blue eyed, broad-built man wearing chainmail and leather armor. His face expressed a lifetime of life on the sea.

As he stood on the prow of the beached ship, he slowly scanned the new land horizon. He saw a broad expanse of fertile grassland, ready to be plowed, seeded, and harvested for crops. In the distance he observed a vast forest of tall, straight trees that would make good timber for his people's homes.

He also saw the smoke rising into the air from a far distant campfire.

He realized that although he and his men had discovered a new land- They were not alone.

1803

Kensington, Minnesota

Olaf Ohman was a slender, red headed, Swedish immigrant that had come to America seeking a fresh start on land that he could call his own. He and his wife Karin had settled in what is now central Minnesota. Olaf had worked hard to make a comfortable life for his wife and son, Edward.

He had recently purchased ten acres of new land from his neighbor, to add to his existing farm, and this morning, he was going to his newly purchased field to clear the grove of trees on it, to be able to cultivate his crops for next season.

Using his team of yoked oxen, he had successfully pulled several of the smaller trees out of the ground and was beginning to work on removal of one of the larger trees. After several attempts, he was finally successful in pulling the resisting tree out of the ground. Unhooking the oxen and getting ready to move on to the next tree, he noticed his son, Edward, using a stick to remove dirt from around the roots of the large, recently pulled tree.

"Edward, stop playing with the dirt. I need you to help me with the next tree," Olaf sternly told his son.

"But papa, there's a funny looking rock in the roots of this tree," his son replied.

"There are a lot of funny looking rocks all over this field," he yelled back, knowing he was going to have to remove each one of them before the newly acquired field would be usable.

"But papa, it looks like there is some kind of writing on this one," his son exclaimed.

That statement caught Olaf by surprise and piqued his curiosity, as he dropped the reins of the oxen and walked over to see what his son was talking about.

Chapter 1

Mark Richards got the text message on his cell phone as he was starting to drive back to Minneapolis.

'Watch her,' was all it said. He knew immediately what it meant as he turned his vehicle around and headed back to Royal Oaks.

Parking his car down the street from Maxine Somers's apartment, he shut the engine off and covered himself from the winter cold with a blanket brought along for just such occasions.

He thought that he was going to have to endure several hours of freezing discomfort before John Randall, his boss, showed up to relieve him from the surveillance. Instead, it was only about a half an hour before Max walked out of her apartment and got into her car. Watching her pull out onto the street, he started his car and tailed her at a discrete distance, trying to keep several vehicles between her and his.

It didn't take him long to figure out where she was going, as she turned onto the road heading toward the Renaissance fair. Knowing her destination, he stayed about a mile behind her, easily keeping her in eyesight. Keeping her in view, as she pulled into the fairgrounds, he drove past the main entrance and proceeded to find a secluded turn off on the side of the road, where he could observe the fair entrance and yet not be easily seen.

He only waited about three quarters of an hour. It was nearing sunset when he spotted Max through his binoculars, leaving the fairgrounds in her car.

Just as he prepared to start following her, a black foreign pickup with a police light bar on its roof and a set of regular Minnesota license plates, passed by his concealed spot, heading in the direction of Max's disappearing car.

That's strange, he thought to himself. *No police department uses that type of truck for patrolling in this area, and no badging on its side door, either.*

Starting to pull his vehicle out of his concealment, he left his lights off and tailed both vehicles at a discreet distance. He watched as the pickup turned on its flashing red and blue strobe lights in order to pull Max's car over. He immediately felt that he knew that the driver in the pickup was Tad Paulson, the rogue cop who was one of the heads of a drug smuggling ring. He had vowed revenge on Max for destroying his gang earlier in the day, and it looked like he was about to carry out his vengeance.

This is going to get messy, Mark thought to himself.

Quietly pulling over unobserved, a good fifty yards behind the two vehicles stopped in front of him, Mark slid over to the passenger side of his SUV and quietly opened the passenger door, hoping the darkness of sunset would conceal his activity. His Navy seal training kicked in as he stealthily but quickly ran down into the ditch and then back up the slope of the embankment on the side of the road so to be even with Max's car. Fortunately, the snow wasn't deep and again fortunately, Paulson was taking his sweet time walking up to Max's car, focusing only on Max's car and not on Mark's movements

Finding concealment behind a six-foot pine tree that was covered with greenery, he was easily able to see Paulson slowly saunter up to Max's car. Mark removed his gun from his holster and brought it up to the firing position. Hearing the pop and snap of a taser that was concealed in Paulson's hand, he knew that he had tasered her, and that there were only seconds to act before he killed her.

In the waning light, the setting sun reflected off Paulson's gun as he pulled it from its holster, to administer the killing shot on the semiconscious Max. Mark knew he had only a second to re-act and quickly stepped out from behind his concealment, hoping it would distract him long enough to get off a shot before Paulson took his.

Mark's sudden movement did its job as Paulson looked up for just a second to see what was moving on the slope. That split second was all Mark needed to get off his shot. As if in slow motion, Mark saw the confused look on Paulson's face as he began raising his weapon at Mark, then Mark's bullet entering his forehead, splattering blood and brain matter all over the side of Max's car.

Pausing for just for a second, Mark ran down the embankment to Max's car. He found her groggy but unharmed, her pistol in her hand. Pulling the taser barbs out of her shoulder, he quickly determined she was okay. Taking his own pistol, he used his handkerchief to wipe all his fingerprints from it and then replaced his gun with the one in Max's hand. He then put her gun in his holster and grabbed the taser and the barb cords from the ground. Quickly ascertaining that Paulson didn't have a taser holster on his belt, he had a final look at Max, who was slowly regaining her wits.

"What? What happened? What are you doing here, Mark?" Max asked groggily, the effects of the taser slowly wearing off.

"Take it easy. It's okay. There will be help here shortly. Just remember this- I wasn't here. I was never here. I'll have help here shortly, but remember this, I wasn't here. Got it?" he explained.

"You weren't here," she parroted, slurring her words. Then noticing the blood spatter on her partially rolled down window, she started panicking, thinking she had been shot. In a panic, she felt her forehead and upper torso to determine where and if she had been shot. Mark stated re-assuredly, "That's not your blood. It's Paulson's. When this is over, you'll be a hero."

"Hero- not here," she repeated back to him, still half dazed.

Mark picked up the taser and ran down the road to his SUV. Looking to see if there was any other traffic on the road, he pulled onto the highway, looking back in his rear-view mirror as he passed the tableau on the side of the highway. After several miles he made an anonymous 911 call to get help for Max and then made a phone call to his boss.

Chapter 2

Maxine Somers woke up alone again in her boyfriend's bed. This was the third day in a row that she had slept in and missed him leaving, early in the morning, and by the time he got home at night, which was usually very late, he was too tired and hungry to do much more than eat and go straight to bed.

Her boyfriend, John Randall, was the owner of a private security company in Minneapolis and was also an undercover agent for a branch of the Federal government. Lately, he had been working on a special project that he refused to tell Maxine anything about. The only thing that Max knew was that it was taking a lot of Randall's time and energy, at a time when she needed him for moral and mental support.

She was the police chief of Royal Oaks, a small town about twenty minutes just outside of Minneapolis. Previously, she had been a beat police officer in Los Angeles, took the detective test and was offered a job in Royal Oaks as the only detective on the small-town police force. When the old chief was killed in a car accident, the mayor of Royal Oaks offered her the job as the new chief, because of her rank and seniority.

It was during that turbulent time of her life, that Max had to deal with a major drug ring headed secretly by a person who she thought was her friend, and also a rogue police officer, who was none other than the police chief's son, Tad Paulson. Tad had planned to take revenge on Max for her destroying his drug ring, by trying to ambush her when she least expected it, and he almost succeeded.

Because of the shooting, Max was suspended from duty for a couple of months by the Royal Oaks mayor, while the State Police and the State Attorney General's office could investigate and rule on the shooting. To Max, the investigation seemed to be taking forever and was slowly taking a toll on Max's emotions and patience.

Why is the investigation taking so long? She thought to herself as she got out of bed. The mayor said it should be concluded in a week or two but so far over eight weeks had passed with no closure in sight.

I need to talk to Mayor Price and find out what's going on, she thought to herself as she took a shower and prepared to start her day. After dressing in her police uniform, she rode the elevator down from Randall's penthouse to the parking garage. The valet service pulled her squad car up for her as she chaffed under the knowledge that her own car was in impound because it might contain evidence related to the shooting of Tad Paulson.

Driving into Royal Oaks, she parked the squad car in her parking place at the police department building. Rather than going inside to communicate with her officers, she decided to walk over to the city office building on foot. The time it took her to get to the mayor's office, gave her the opportunity to formulate the questions she would be asking him again about the investigation, and why it was taking so long.

Arriving at the mayor's office, his secretary had her wait for a few minutes as she notified the mayor that Max was there to see him. Mayor Price shortly came out and ushered Max into his office, telling his secretary to hold his calls. Closing the door to his office, he signaled for Max to take a seat.

Sitting down, Max took a long, deep breath in preparation for her speech to the mayor, but before she could start, the mayor began speaking first.

"I know what you're going to say, so let me save you the trouble," he opened the conversation with, catching Max off guard. "This investigation has been taking way too long," he continued.

"What seems to be the problem now, Sir?" Max questioned, relieved that she didn't have to start the conversation.

"Well," the mayor started by saying, "the investigation seems to have hit an impasse."

"Impasse? What kind of impasse? The State Highway Patrol did a complete investigation and found no problem. The county Grand Jury did a complete investigation and found no problem. What in creation is causing an impasse?" Max pleaded, trying to stay calm but her frustration and emotions started to betray her in her voice.

"Not what but who," the mayor responded. "It seems that the State Attorney General, Ted Russell, wants to make an example of dirty police in Minnesota. He wants to hang someone, anyone he can, to bolster up his re-election campaign."

"And I'm the someone?" Max questioned.

"You're the someone," the mayor concurred.

"How did I get so lucky," Max responded dejectedly, slumping back into the chair.

"Look Maxine, you're a good cop and an excellent chief of police. All I want, all I ask of you to do is go and talk to him. That's all. Just tell him what happened like you told the Highway Patrol investigators and the Grand Jury. If you play nice with him, I'm sure he'll realize that there is nothing he can hang on you. Just go, be good, tell your story, and get this over with." Mayor Price pleaded.

"And if I don't?" Max questioned, knowing full well what the response would be.

"He's prepared to subpoena you," the mayor stated in a matter-of-fact tone.

"So, if I understand correctly, either I can resign and be prosecuted, or go and talk to this Ted Russell and maybe I'll save my job, or possibly face criminal charges if he doesn't believe me. Right?" Max questioned despondently, feeling like she was falling into a dark hole.

"That's about it in a nutshell," the mayor concurred. "Look, let me set up an appointment for you. You just go and explain everything as it happened, He has the evidentiary proceedings on record so if you just fill in any gaps in the information he wants, then I'm sure you'll be back at work very soon. Okay?

Max sat in her chair for a few moments, thinking over her options. She loved her job and the people she worked with. Thinking over her situation for several seconds, she finally responded. "Okay, I'll go and talk to him. Anything to get back to work if you think it will help."

"Good," the mayor responded, rising from his chair. "Right decision. I'll set everything up with his office and get back to you with the where and when. I'll call you soon." Going over to Max, he took her hand and shook it warmly. Max recognized that this was the signal that the meeting was over and started for the door of the mayor's office. As she reached the door, she stopped, paused, and asked him, "Is this the last impasse, mayor?"

"I hope so Maxine. I certainly hope so. I don't want to lose any more personnel in the police department." he responded, as he opened the door for Max.

"Me either, mayor. Me either," as she slowly walked out the door.

Chapter 3

Max left the mayor's office and walked slowly back to her car. She thought about stopping into the police department and checking on what was happening there, but in the end decided not to. Instead, she went over to her apartment and checked on it to make sure everything was okay and to pick up her mail.

It's a good thing I don't have any pets, plants, or a goldfish, because they would have died from starvation for as much as I've been home lately. She thought to herself. It didn't take long to check things out in her apartment. It all looked exactly the same as when she was last there over five weeks ago. Everything looked good except for a layer of dust covering her furniture and a vase of dead flowers that Randall had sent her many, many weeks ago.

Vowing to herself to move back to her own apartment and clean it when she had more time, she proceeded to go over to the apartment complex mailboxes and pick up her mail. Finding her mailbox key took a few second as she hadn't used it much in the past. Opening the mailbox, she was surprised at how full it was. It was so stuffed that it took several attempts to get it all out. Spotting a plastic grocery sack in the garbage bin next to the mailboxes, she picked it up and used the bag to hold all of her mail so she could easily carry it to the car.

On her way back to Randall's penthouse in Minneapolis, she couldn't help but mull over in her mind all the events that had transpired over the last few months, and how much her life had changed with becoming the police chief of Royal Oaks.

Arriving at the building of Randall's penthouse, she left the squad car for the valet to park and then headed up the elevator to Randall's penthouse. Once there, she threw her jacket on the sofa and the bag of mail onto the kitchen counter and headed into the bedroom to change out of her uniform. In the bedroom, she was surprised to see Randall sprawled out on the bed, sound asleep.

Trying to be as quiet as possible, she silently took off her uniform and started going through the closet for a comfortable sweatshirt and a pair of jeans. Once she found what she was looking for, she decided to put them on in the living room so she wouldn't disturb Randall's afternoon nap.

Walking out of the closet, holding her change of clothes, she was surprised to see Randall laying on the bed, awake and looking at her with a smug grin on his face.

"I was having a great dream about you and when I woke up, there you were," he said patting the edge of the mattress and sliding over so she had a spot to sit. Taking the hint, she dropped her clothes she was carrying on the floor and went over and sat on the mattress where Randall had indicated.

Randall reached over to her, wrapped his arms around her, pulled her to him and gave her a passionate kiss. She responded by lying down next to him and kissing him back.

"Nice to see you, stranger. You home for a while?" she asked hopefully.

"The whole day and the whole night, and I really do need to make up some time with you," he replied, holding her tighter.

"Yes, you do, and we're going to start right now, Sir," she whispered passionately back.

Randall replied by grabbing her around the waist and pulling her on top of him.

"My pleasure," he responded, kissing her again.

"And mine to," she eagerly replied, enjoying the warmth of his touch and kisses.

Several hours later, Max awoke to the sounds of Randall moving around in the kitchen. Feeling alive and refreshed for the first time in several weeks, she threw on her clothes that were still laying on the floor where she had dropped them and headed out to join him there. Randall, seeing her walking up to him, turned, grabbed her around the waist and pulled her close to him. Planting a playful kiss on her neck, she quickly pulled from him, turning her head away.

"With a look of surprise, Randall asked, "What's wrong?"

"You need a shave, John, and a shower-bad," she replied, wrinkling up her nose.

"You didn't object a few hours ago," he responded, slightly offended.

"That was then. This is now. What are you doing in the kitchen?" she asked, looking around.

"In case you didn't notice, it's almost seven o'clock in the evening, and I was getting a little hungry, so I thought I would whip us up something for supper," Replied Randall.

"Did I sleep that long?" Max queried. Randall shook his head in the affirmative.

Thinking for a few seconds, she replied, "I'll make us something while you go shave and shower. Okay?"

"Deal," he replied, heading off to the bathroom. It wasn't much later that she heard the sound of the shower running.

Max turned her attention to making supper for them. Just as she was putting the finishing touches on the meal, Randall came back into the kitchen looking and smelling much better.

"How did your meeting go with the mayor?" he asked her nonchalantly as he sat on the stool at the breakfast bar.

"How did you know I went to see the mayor?" she asked incredulously, staring at him.

"A little bird told me," he responded coyly.

"No, really, how did you know?" she shot back, slightly irritated.

Seeing that she was getting agitated, he explained, "I was at the courthouse getting some permits for the Renaissance project when you walked right past me. You looked like you were on a mission, so I decided to leave you to it. Then you went down the hall of the mayor's office. So, I then knew where you were headed."

"The Renaissance? Your special project is for Foley?" She asked.

"Yup," was all Randall replied, as he took another bite of food.

"But I didn't think you started doing your security work there until the fall season? It's only spring." Max queried.

"I don't, but my security company has a contract for some special work for him, and Foley requested that I handle it personally. You know- when you want the best- hire the best," he replied smiling back at her. "You know- this omelet is really delicious," he said, taking another bite and smiling, knowing that he had perked Max's interest.

Max had taken the bait and started pressing him for more details. "What kind of project?" she asked, "and by the way, it's really hard to mess up a vegetable, mushroom omelet," she added.

Randall just smiled back at her, as he took another bite. After swallowing his mouthful of omelet, he replied, "Foley is going to try and make the Renaissance more profitable by expanding the season and making it a destination venue. He's been enlarging the area, putting in a medieval chapel, adding more shops, a medieval motel, more parking, and my special project."

"Which is?" Max questioned curiously.

"Special- special and secret." Randall replied, picking up the dishes from the breakfast bar, rinsing them, and putting them in the dishwasher along with the skillet from the stove. He started wiping down the counter until he got to the bag of mail that Max had brought back from her apartment.

"What's this?" he asked, pointing at the bag, trying to change the subject.

"My mail from the apartment. I checked it after my meeting with mayor Price, this morning," Max replied.

"By the way, how did your meeting go?" he questioned.

"Not good," Max responded curtly.

"Why? What happened?" Randall asked, sensing the tension in her voice.

"I now have to go and see a Ted Russell, sometime this week," Max replied sullenly.

"Ted Russell? Like the State Attorney General, Ted Russell?" Randall stated surprisingly.

"Yes- why? Do you know him?" Max asked.

"Yah- he's been to my annual company Christmas party a few times in the past. Be careful around him," Randall advised warningly.

"Why?" Max queried.

"Because he's a shark. If you're not careful, he'll eat you alive. He's one of the movers and shakers in Minnesota politics with his eyes on moving up the political ladder. Some say he has his target on the governorship," he explained to her.

"Mayor Price said that he's up for re-election and that he might use my head as a trophy to get there," Max lamented.

"He'll do it in a heartbeat if he can. Look- do you want me to make some calls to Washington and have some of my people yank his chain?" asked Randall, starting to go through the sack of Max's mail.

"No, I want to handle this myself," she stated firmly.

Going through the bag, Randall finally pulled out one of the political advertisements from the pile and placed it in front of Max. "Here's who you'll be seeing," he said, pointing to the picture on the flyer. The photo that Max saw printed on the brochure was that of an older, puggy man, with thinning gray hair, and deep blue eyes.

He looks like somebody's grandfather, Max thought to herself.

As if Randall was reading her mind, he commented, "Don't let his looks fool you; he's one of the best lawyers in Minnesota, and he can smell if you're lying to him."

"I have no intentions of lying to him. Why would I?" Max shot back. Max knew that Randall was aware of the real circumstances of Tad Paulson's shooting, but nothing was ever discussed about it between them.

"No reason. I just wanted to forewarn you, that's all," Randall responded cautiously, realizing that Max was becoming agitated.

Trying to change the subject, he started going through the rest of the mail on the counter, finally pulling out a small white envelope that had been covered by the other bills and political ads that made up most of her mail,

"Looks like a personal letter for you," he stated, showing it to Max.

Puzzled, Max took the envelope from him, opened it, and read the contents. "Looks like Ms. Nelson from the Renaissance fair is getting married this summer. This is a save the date for the middle of July," she stated out loud, as she reread the note.

"That was nice of her to invite you," Randall replied nonchalantly. "I had heard rumors that she had got engaged earlier this year. I guess they finally set a date."

"Looks that way," Max responded.

Chapter 4

Max got the morning phone call later that week from the mayor, informing her that the appointment had been set with the State Attorney General's office in St. Paul, for that same afternoon. Max was grateful, as it didn't give her much time to worry about how the meeting would go. *Ignorance is bliss.* She thought to herself.

After lunch, she put on her uniform and drove across the river into St. Paul, and then on to the state capital building, where her meeting was scheduled to take place. Clearing the security guards and locating Ted Russell's office only took a few minutes. The secretary in the front office verified her appointment and asked her to take a seat, as Mr. Russell was running behind schedule, apologizing that it might be fifteen or twenty minutes more before he could see her. After about thirty minutes the secretary told Max that she could go in. Max felt like her stomach was going to be upset from her nerves on edge.

Walking into the magnificent office, Max saw several men sitting around a large wooden conference desk. All the men rose from their chairs as she walked in. The man that Max recognized as Ted Russell walked over to her, shook her hand, welcomed her, and escorted her to a vacant chair at the table. After she was seated, Ted Russell started speaking to Max and the group of men.

"We would like to thank you for joining us on such short notice, Chief Somers, and we would also like to thank you for your military service to our country, and your service to our great state of Minnesota," He opened with.

Then turning to the rest of the men, he continued. "Gentlemen, this is the little lady who brought down one of the major drug rings in our state, after being tortured and left for dead."

After making his short speech, he began applauding and was quickly joined by the other men in the room, as they all rose in unison. After the applause subsided and the men sat down, Ted Russell, who had remained standing, addressed Max and the group of men again.

"Gentlemen," then turning to Max, he continued, "and Chief Somers, I would like to take this moment to personally thank you for your service as a Minnesota police officer, for your outstanding heroism and valor, and your dedication to duty, by presenting you with an accommodation for your above and beyond service to our great state of Minnesota."

He then handed her a rolled-up parchment, with the proclamation on it.

All Max could do was just sit in her chair, stunned, as everybody in the room rose and applauded her again. As they continued applauding, the side door of the office opened, and several other people entered the room. Some of the people began taking photos and others set up TV cameras. It didn't take long for Max to figure out that the meeting was a media set up to present her with the accommodation. Red faced with embarrassment, all she could do was stand next to the Attorney General, with the other men from the room on either side of her, and smile for the cameras as the reporters shot questions to her and Ted Russell. Trying to keep her composure, she answered them as best she could. Finally, after about twenty minutes, the Attorney General brought the questions to an end and asked the reporters to finish up. As the reporters and the council members were leaving the room, he walked over to Max and whispered to her, "Can you stay behind for a few minutes? I would like to ask you a question in private."

Nodding her head in affirmation, she waited until everybody but the two of them had left the conference room. As the door closed with the last person exiting, she sat down on one of the chairs, waiting for the question that was coming. Ted Russell came over and sat down next to her, giving her a minute to absorb everything that had happened in the last half hour.

"I'm sorry for the deception, Chief Somers. "And no- your mayor was not in or aware of this award. Everything he told you, he believed to be true. This whole plan for your accommodation was my doing, and I'm sorry if this put any emotional stress or strain on you," he stated apologetically.

"Well, you certainly did surprise me. I thought I came here to lose my job. But tell me, why all this secrecy?" she asked, curiously.

"I want you to endorse my campaign for re-election," he stated bluntly, pausing to let the statement sink in.

"Even though you might not know it, your apprehension of the Royal Oaks drug ring made you a type of folk hero around here, and with the law enforcement community of this state. It seems my campaign is not going as well as I had hoped, and I need a major endorsement from someone like you to help push me over the top."

He continued, "You are going to be on all the major local and network news stations tonight and probably tomorrow as well, along with your face and story in all the local newspapers. I need someone like you to endorse me and help raise my election ratings," he paused, then continued.

"Well? Tell me, what do you think? Can I count on you?"

Max thought about it for a moment or two.

"I'm going to have to think about it, for a while," Max stated, not sure as to what her next move might be. "It's a big jump from a local police chief to a folk hero," she said, smiling. "I think I'm going to have to weigh my options on this matter. When do I have to give you an answer?" she asked.

"Look, think about it for a couple of weeks. I'll have my assistant call you at the end of that time to get your answer," he replied. "Please give it your consideration as it could be greatly beneficial to your city and to your career. Understand?" he stated, emphasizing the word 'career.'

"Yes- I understand," Max replied, fully aware of the implications that were veiled in his statement. "Does that mean I'm back on the job?" she added, hopefully.

"It certainly does. I'll call your mayor today and inform him so," he said, rising from the chair, and shaking Max's hand as he escorted her to the door. "Think about this offer long and hard," he suggested, as he held the door open for her. "But not too long."

Max stood outside the office door after it had closed, thinking over what had just happened in the office. Finally, the secretary, who was watching Max standing there, commented, "Congratulations, Chief Somers."

"Thank you," she replied as she was interrupted from her thoughts. "Thank you very much," she repeated as she headed out of the building and back to Randall's apartment, her accommodation in hand.

Chapter 5

The trip back to Randall's place only took a half an hour. This gave Max an opportunity to think over the proposition the Attorney General had given her. In the end, she decided to talk with Randall about it, along with discussing it with Mayor Price, before making her final decision in the matter.

Arriving at the penthouse, she found Randall gone again. Changing out of her uniform and back into street clothes, she decided to drive to Royal Oaks and try to see if the mayor was available, as it was getting late into the afternoon.

She was absentmindedly driving and thinking over her options when something instinctively snapped her out of her revery. Something caught her eye in her car's rear-view mirror. She had the uneasy feeling that a black pickup with heavily tinted windows about a half a mile behind was following her. At first, she just put it off to nerves but as she proceeded down the highway, she observed as she slowed down, the other vehicle slowed down and as she sped up, so too, did the other vehicle, maintaining a constant distance between them and her.

Finally, as she pulled into Royal Oaks city limit, she observed from her rear-view mirror, the following pickup turn left and exit the highway. Breathing a sigh of relief, she put the whole incident down as a case of nerves.

Arriving at city hall, she parked her car and went looking for the mayor. His secretary let her into his office almost immediately. Rising as she entered his office, he started the conversation before Max could even open her mouth.

"Honest to God, Maxine, I had no idea Russell was going to do that. He had me snowballed along with you the whole time. I got the phone call from his office about fifteen minutes ago, telling me what transpired," the mayor explained, apologetically.

Sitting down in the chair in front of the desk, she commented, "Did he tell you he wants me to be the poster child for his campaign?"

"No, he completely failed to mention that part. Really?" the mayor asked incredulously.

"What did you tell him?"

"I told him I had to think on it. I have a couple of weeks to make my decision and I wanted to get your input on what I should to. I also want to get back to work as soon as possible, with your permission, of course," Max explained.

The mayor sat silent for a minute or two and then responded, "No and yes. No, I wouldn't do it in support for him, and yes, you can get back to work."

"Explain," Max countered. "Why not the support?"

"Well, for a couple of reasons. First, he is on the ropes as far as his campaign is going, and second, I don't think our police department should get involved in politics," he replied.

"I can understand not involving the department in politics, but what do you mean, 'On the ropes?' I thought he was a shoe in for re-election," Max questioned.

The mayor sat back in his chair for a moment or two and then replied, "In past years, that was certainly true. But this year, he is facing a new, up and comer of an opponent that just might knock him out of office. This is someone who is out spending him over two to one on advertising and has a real appeal to the younger voters. She just might be able to beat the old bastard."

"She?" Max queried.

"Yup!" the mayor replied, smiling at the fact that he had perked up Max's curiosity. "Assumpta Morgan is her name, and she has exploded on to the Minnesota political scene with a lot of new ideas, a lot of money and a lot of appeal to the young voters, as well as a lot of the older voters. People figure she is going to be a real force to contend with in the political field, now and in the future."

"Assumpta? That's an odd name," Max commented to the mayor.

"It's an old name from Ireland, I think," he replied. "Probably a family name."

"Anyway," he said, continuing, "I really think and suggest you might want to stay out of politics for now, and get back to work. How does that sound, Chief?"

It only took a second for Max to reply, "Fantastic- I can't wait to get back to my job. Can I possibly start today?"

"Sure, but it's getting kind of late," he stated, looking at his watch. "Why don't you get a good night's rest and start tomorrow? Your plate is going to be full for the next week or two," the mayor replied.

"How so?" Max asked.

"Well, you know you're down a detective and a patrol officer, what with your promotion and losing Paulson. I wanted to wait on replacing anybody until you got re-instated and back on the job so you would have a say in the hiring process. It seems only fair that you have the final say in building your police department personnel. By the way, I think your assistant chief is more than ready for you to get back," the mayor said, smiling.

"How is Mark Wilson doing? He really got a load dumped on him these last few months," Max asked.

"Officer Wilson has been doing a stellar job. He's kept everything together and has even been taking some detective certification courses at the University of Minnesota. I think he might be angling for your old job as detective," the mayor replied, slyly.

"I'll keep that in mind when I do the interviewing," Max shot back to him, with a smile on her face. "But if he gets promoted to detective, that means I'll be down two officers. Right?"

"Huh? Right," the mayor replied, scratching his head while trying to figure out how Max had manipulated him. "Wait, that can't be right," he started saying, but before he could protest any more, Max started heading out the door."

"Thanks Mayor. I'll be on the job starting in the morning. And thanks for all your advice and help," she stated, as she quickly headed out of the mayor's office.

"Don't forget to get your car out of impound," the mayor stated, as Max headed out to the hallway. Max raised her hand with a thumbs up in response to the mayor's last statement.

Chapter 6

The mayor was right. It didn't take Max long to get back to work. She passionately believed that a police force should represent its community, and since half the population was female, then half of a police force should be female. However, she was also enough of a realist to know that the new deputies she would hire wouldn't both be women but felt that a least one more woman on the force would help to drag her department into the twenty first century.

Arriving early the next morning at the Royal Oaks police department, the first person to greet her was her deputy chief, Mark Wilson. He and Max were the only ones who had arrived early before the shift change.

"It's good you see you back, Chief," he stated, as Max walked through the door into the squad room.

"Glad to be back," she replied, walking over to the coffee pot, and pouring some of it into a Styrofoam cup. Taking a sip, she almost spit it out, exclaiming, "God, that is still the worst coffee I've ever tasted." Smiling, she continued, "Glad things haven't changed a bit since I've been gone." Sitting on the corner of one of the desks in the room, she asked, "What's been happening, Mark?"

Deputy Wilson poured some coffee and joined Max, sitting on another desk corner across from her. "Not much. The coffee is still terrible, and crime is still boring as hell around here. Mostly traffic problems and kids shoplifting at the new mall. That's what is keeping us busy," he commented.

Max took another sip of the coffee and continued, "I hear you're taking night classes and doing a good job on keeping a lid on things around here."

Mark blushed slightly as he took a sip of his coffee. "You've been talking to the mayor, haven't you?" Max nodded her head in affirmation and continued drinking,

"I thought it wouldn't hurt since no one knew for sure when you'd be back. I hope you're not upset," he stated, almost apologetically.

"No, not in the least. In fact, I applaud you for taking the initiative and I think that the position of deputy chief is yours permanently, if you want it," Max concluded.

"Want it? Yes, sure I want it," he replied as he hastily rose from the desk. "I'd be honored to be the Deputy Chief of Royal Oaks and work with you."

"Any idea for your assistant?" she asked him.

"Well, deputy Curtis Jenkins has been assisting me while you've been gone. He's got the experience and the know-how. I think he would work out well," Wilson explained.

Max stood and shook his hand, replying, "Great. We can make the announcements at shift change this morning and I'll inform the mayor of your promotion."

By this time, many of the of the other deputies started arriving at the squad room for the morning shift change. After the announcement of the promotions, and the soon to be added new deputies, the men of the different shifts headed out into the field or home, leaving Max and a couple of officers in the shift room.

It didn't take Max long to settle back into the routine of police work in Royal Oaks. After several hours of paperwork in her office, she finally decided to take a lunch break and head over to the new shopping mall that had just opened several weeks earlier. Driving through main street of Royal Oaks on her way to the mall, she welcomed the warm, spring sunshine coming through her car window. She saw that the winter snow that had covered the ground for so long was almost completely melted, and large spots of green foliage was poking through the ground in various places. *Thankfully, winter seemed to be over, and spring finally arrived,* thought Max to herself.

Arriving at the mall parking lot, she parked in the spot reserved for police cars and spent several hours having lunch and walking through the hallways of the building, marveling that such a small town of Royal Oaks could support such a large shopping mall.

After her lunch and exploring the mall, she decided it was time to call it a day. Calling Mark to have him cover for her, she headed back into Minneapolis. Now that she was back at work, she realized that her days of staying at Randall's penthouse were coming to an end, and she would have to start residing in her own apartment. She felt a sense of sadness, as she had really enjoyed her stay with Randall, when he was around. During the drive back to Minneapolis, she felt a sense of melancholy and finality. She realized that this was the start of a new chapter in her life, and she was determined to enjoy it as much as she could.

I have a great job, a fantastic man in my life and a daughter who is working hard and staying in college, she thought to herself as she headed for the city. *What more can I ask for?*

Arriving at Randall's penthouse, she realized that he wasn't home, so she started going through her things to decide what to leave and what to take back to her apartment in Royal Oaks. After about fifteen minutes of organizing, she heard the front door open.

"You decent?" Randall shouted so that Max could hear him in the back bedroom.

"Yeah, just going through my stuff to take back to Royal Oaks this weekend," she replied.

Walking into the bedroom, Randall gave her a hug and a kiss on her cheek. "Getting ready to move out?" he asked. "You must be getting tired of me already," he said teasingly.

"No," she replied. "I just need to get back to my apartment. This driving back and forth is really starting to wear on me. I thought Saturday would be the best day to make the move."

"Speaking of Saturday, would you like some help moving? I'll be free all weekend," he stated.

"You're done with your Renaissance project?" she asked, as she turned to face him.

"Sure am, and I'm turning it over to Foley this weekend. I thought I could help you move, and then take you out there and show the project to you. Maybe catch a bite afterward. What do you think?" he asked, hoping she'd say yes.

"Sounds fantastic," she replied, turning to face him. Let me finish here and then I'll start supper."

Then putting her arms around his neck, she gave him a kiss. "I'm going to miss all of this, and especially you," she said with a whisper.

Randall reciprocated by kissing her back and whispered to her, "and I'm going to miss not having you here with me."

As Max slipped out of his arms and headed out of the bedroom, she stated, "You take a shower and I'll start supper. Then we can say our goodbyes afterward. Deal?"

"Deal," Randall replied with a smile, knowing full well, how the evening was going to progress.

Chapter 7

Saturday started as a beautiful, warm Minnesota June day. Not too hot, not too cold. Very little humidity, with white puffy clouds in the sky, and thankfully, no mosquitoes. Max could almost smell the spring freshness in the air as she walked out of the elevator of Randall's townhouse and into the parking garage.

This is going to be the start of a new beginning for me and my job. She thought to herself. She was excited to start work again, and that Randall was finally able to spend some quality time with her. She had on a pair of jean shorts and a tank top, with her hair pulled back in a ponytail. Randall had on his favorite jeans and a tee shirt that was just snug enough to show off his muscular torso.

"Looking good, boyfriend," she commented to him as he got into his SUV.

"Not too bad yourself, girlfriend. Showing off a lot of skin today. I hope you don't get too sunburned out at the Renaissance," he replied.

"Got it covered," she said smiling, pulling a bottle of suntan lotion out of her purse.

"Great, good to go?" he asked.

Max scanned the back of the SUV that contained her suitcase and several boxes of her stuff.

"Yup. Good to go," she replied.

It took forty- five minutes for them to get to Max's apartment in Royal Oaks and another ten minutes for them to unload the SUV of Max's belongings. Once done with that task, it was off to the Renaissance site. On the way, Randall asked her if she had brought her PTSD medication. Max dug into her purse and pulled out the plastic pill bottle and then shook it to show Randall there were pills in it.

"Why do you ask?" she questioned; her curiosity piqued.

"They're burning a lot of wood and trees on the site, and I know your PTSD trigger is smoke in the air. I just wanted you prepared so you don't have an episode, once we get there," he explained.

"Thanks for the heads up," she responded, taking a pill out of the container, putting it in her mouth and chasing it with coffee from the Thermos located between the seat, "Forewarned is forearmed."

The rest of the trip was spent in relative silence until they approached the spot on the road where Max had been ambushed by Tad Paulson, the rogue police officer who was involved with a drug cartel. He had tried to ambush her as she was leaving the Renaissance site. As Tad went for his gun, he was himself ambushed by Mark Wilson, Randall's associate at Randall Security.

"Are you okay?" Randall asked, seeing the look of consternation on Max's face as they passed the spot on the highway.

"Yah, I'm fine," she replied pensively, secretly wishing that she wouldn't ever have to face the memory again but knowing that she would.

After several more minutes, they pulled into the Renaissance fair grounds. Randall informed her, "We're here," attempting to break the silence between them. Max looked around, trying to spot the differences from when she was last there. Randall had told her that everything had been changed around or improved. Even the parking lot had been expanded. Many of the trees from the parking lot area had been cut down and burnt. Most of the piles of ash from the burnt trees still smoldered around different places in the newly cleared parking lot. To Max it looked almost double in size from what it was last fall. There were several cars and pickups along with a black limo parked by the entrance gates with a driver sitting inside it. Walking up to the front entrance, she noticed that even the entrance gates had been expanded and given a fresh coat of paint.

"Wow! Looks like Foley really spent some big bucks on the upgrades," Max stated, looking around at the changes.

"It's not just Oliver Foley anymore. He's got some new partners with deep pockets and new ideas, who are footing most of the improvements. I can't wait for you to see what's been done inside the gates," he said eagerly, grabbing Max's hand and taking her through the gate stile, into the new Renaissance fair.

Chapter 8

Randall was right. Once though the gate, Max was amazed at the changes made. Instead of the old, dilapidated vendor's stalls, new buildings had been erected that looked like they were truly built in the fifteen or sixteenth century. All of the buildings had two stories, the ground level was space for the merchant to sell the wares, while the top level appeared to be quarters for the merchants who stay on site when the fair was open for the expanded season. Each of the buildings was painted in a variety of colors, which were purposely distressed to make them appear authentic Renaissance structures. All of the buildings had thatched roofs that lent even more to the realistic appearance.

In the middle court, where the old water wheel had been, there was a beautiful, small chapel with open walls, stained glass panels, and a heavily thatched roof, surrounded by flowering vines and rose bushes. Several stone benches were located by the chapel doorway.

"Wow- they have really pulled out the stops in improving the site!" Max exclaimed as she looked around at all the changes.

"That's just the old section. Wait till you see the new section," Randall excitedly replied, as he guided Max down the gravel pathway to the new area at the far end of the grounds.

Approaching the new expanded area, Max saw a massive wall built of logs, sticking vertically in the ground. Each log was sharpened on its end and rose about fifteen feet into the air. In the middle section of the wall was a set of double gates made from the same type of logs and wide enough for seven or eight people to comfortably walk through side by side when fully open. On either side of the gates were wooden watchtowers rising about another ten feet above the top of the palisade. Max could tell that a lot of time and money had been spent in building this structure.

"Looks like something out of an old cowboy and Indian movie," Max commented aloud, as they walked through the gates.

"Right concept, wrong time," Randall explained as he walked with Max down the gravel road leading to a series of what could only be described as medieval huts. Each hut seemed to be made of mud walls and thatched roofs, with a single door on the front of each dwelling. Some had windows but most did not. Rising above all the huts further on was a massive structure about forty feet wide and about two hundred feet long. Towering almost thirty feet into the air, the front of the structure had a set of double doors made from wood planks. The doors were over twelve feet tall, with all kinds of intricate whorls and spirals carved into them. Max was definitely impressed.

"Ever been in a Viking long house?" Randall asked her, excitedly.

"No," she replied.

"Well, you will now," he exclaimed, as he pulled opened the huge doors.

Max heard the hinges groan as the doors slowly opened to admit them. Up until this time, Max hadn't seen another person anywhere on the grounds.

Entering the building, it took a couple of seconds for her eyes to adjust from the bright sunlight outside to the dim lighting in the long house. She then discerned a group of people having a conversation about halfway into the building. As she and Randall got closer to the people, she started to recognize several of the individuals in the group. Oliver Foley, the owner, and manager of the fair was having a discussion with a woman and two men. Next to him was Ms. Nelson, Foley's personal assistant.

Ms. Nelson was first to see Max and Randall walking up to them. "They're here," she exclaimed.

"It's about time," Oliver Foley responded, irritation resonating in his voice. "We had to start the presentation without you. Let me introduce you to everyone."

Pointing to Randall, he proceeded with the introductions, "John Randall, head of security here and also owner of Randall Security in Minneapolis." Then turning to Max, "This is the Chief of Police of Royal Oaks, Maxine Somers."

Then he turned to the woman, and stated, "I'd like you to meet Assumpta Morgan and her brother, Lars Morgan, and this gentleman is their personal assistant, Mr. Jonathan Smith. The Morgan's are the major investors in the fair and thanks to them, all of the upgrades and improvements were possible."

Max acknowledged each of them but was really struck by the beauty of the woman. She appeared to be around thirty years old, about five feet tall, with long straight black hair and dark penetrating eyes. She wore a tailored black pants suit with no blouse on underneath. The hair, eyes and suit contrasted and accentuated her smooth, white flawless skin.

Max could almost feel some type of magnetic power coming from Assumpta. It was like she was an old soul in a young body. She had the feeling that Assumpta's dark eyes could look right into a person's mind and soul and read them like a book. Max was both fascinated, yet slightly scared of her. She also wondered if others could feel the same about Assumpta or was it just she who felt it.

Her brother, Lars, was the complete opposite. Almost six and a half feet tall, tan and built like a body builder. He had long blonde hair and deep blue eyes. He reminded Max of a model, or one of those professional wrestlers seen on television.

Shaking Max's hand, and seeing the look on Max's face, Assumpta explained, as if she was reading her mind, "Same father but different mothers." Then taking Randall's hand in greeting, she added, "So glad to see you again, John. It been a real pleasure working with you and your company." Max thought that Assumpta held Randall's hand a little longer than she liked.

Mr. Smith then shook Randall's and Max's hands, Max thought that his hand was cold as ice. Dressed in a brown suit, Smith looked to be about six feet tall and of average build and when he shook Max's hand, she could see the strapping of a shoulder holster under his jacket. Max didn't say anything.

After everyone had been introduced, Assumpta bluntly asked Max, catching her off guard,

"I hear that Ted Russell is working you for his Attorney General endorsement,"

With that question, Max realized where she had heard Assumpta's name before. She was the opponent running against Ted Russell. The one that the mayor told her about. Momentarily taken back at the realization of who she was, Max carefully replied, "Yes, he asked me to endorse him."

"Well, I hate to be nosey, but may I ask what you told him?" she asked in a polite way that Max didn't find intrusive.

"Nothing yet, but I have decided that I'm staying out of politics," she stated flatly.

"That's a shame. We need more strong women in politics these days," Assumpta responded curtly.

Max tried hard to not like her but couldn't.

Chapter 9

Max patiently listened to the conversation between Foley, Randall, and the others. From their conversation, she figured out that the new section of the fair was designed to be a living history museum, with a group of demonstrators living and reconstructing what medieval life was like. The huts that they had passed earlier were the living quarters for the demonstrators during the time the fair was open. Although the huts appeared to be made of mud, they really were constructed out of concrete with waterproof, wooden roofs covered with a layer of thatch. The long house they were standing in was designed as a space for demonstrators and artisans to demonstrate and sell goods to the visiting public.

Oliver Foley told the group that he had negotiated with an organization called the Society of Viking Research to take over the site, and to supply the overall ambiance for the Viking portion of the area. Randall questioned if it was wise to limit the demonstrations to such a narrow period when the Renaissance time period was a much later time in history.

"It's called the Renaissance fair, but the Vikings were running around in the eight hundred; the Renaissance started in the sixteen hundred. Don't you think that's a little confusing?"

"Got it covered," Oliver Foley explained. "We are rebranding the site as the Medieval fair. That way we have the whole spectrum of time from the Dark Ages through the Renaissance time period covered."

"Makes good sense," Randall stated. "Bigger time frame, bigger audience appeal." Then asking, "Have you inspected the special exhibit yet?"

We were just getting ready to look at it when you arrived," Assumpta replied.

Taking Max's hand, Randall and the others started walking down the length of the long house until they got to what Max thought was four large rectangular shaped rocks standing upright. Each rock was about thirty inches thick, stood about eight feet from the ground and had Celtic carvings on it, covering each of its four sides. The rocks were placed in such a way that they formed a square about ten feet in length. In the middle of the square was a fifth rock, shaped in a more roundish form with a flat surface on its top about three feet from the ground. Covering the middle rock was a square box made from what appeared to be thick glass. It surrounded the center rock and rose into the air as high as the four rocks surrounding it. Spotlights concealed in the ceiling illuminated the center, almost forcing the eye to focus solely on the flat surface of the center rock.

Max was impressed but confused and whispered in Randall's ear. "Impressive, but what is it?"

Randall smiled and whispered back, "My special project."

Just then Oliver Foley spoke up. "Mr. Randall, you're sure that this is ready?"

"Very sure," Randall replied as he took out his cell phone and hit a couple of buttons on it. Picking up a small piece of construction wood from the ground, he handed it to Foley and said, "Throw it in."

Foley took the wood and threw it in so that it hit the plexiglass cover on the center rock. Immediately an alarm sounded that was so loud that Max had to cover her ears. The noise from the alarm was deafening and started to give her a headache. Max had to put her hands over her ears to try and alleviate the noise.

Randall then pushed a button on his phone that shut off the alarm. With silence restored, he explained, "There are proximity sensors camouflaged in the four sentinel stones along with a touch sensor on the three-inch bulletproof Lucite cover. The base of the platform is sunk into four feet of re-enforced concrete, and not only does the alarm go off here but also at the security center. There are video cameras located in the ceiling throughout the whole building.so that every inch of this building is covered."

"Thank you for the demonstration, Mr. Randall," Oliver interrupted. "See- you hire the best, you get the best." Addressing the other three people he turned away from Max and Randall. This gave Max the opportunity to question Randall.

"Why all this security for a rock and a glass cover?" she questioned.

"Well, technically it's not a rock. Everything here is really cast concrete disguised to look like ancient rocks. Pretty convincing-right?"

Max nodded in affirmation. "But why all the time and expense of securing a fake rock with a plexiglass cover over it?" she questioned again.

"It's not the rock but what's going to be sitting on it," he replied as he and Max walked back over and joined the others.

Chapter 10

With the demonstration over, the group began the walk back to the parking lot. On the way, Ms. Nelson strolled along side Max. When they got to the new chapel area, Ms. Nelson took Max's hand and led her to the front of the chapel. The others kept on walking. There was a bench in front of the building where they both sat down.

Ms. Nelson started the conversation. "I hope you got my note for my wedding?" she began. Max nodded in affirmation. Nelson continued, "I wanted to tell you, thanks for helping me get through my troubles with the arson charges concerning Simon Foley."

Simon Foley was the brother of her boss, Oliver Foley. Simon was blackmailing Ms. Nelson with photos of when he drugged and slept with her, threatening to tell her fiancé and her boss, Oliver.

Simon Foley and his wife were part of a drug cartel and were murdered by Tad Paulson when they tried to quit the cartel and leave Royal Oaks. Tad shot and killed both of them in their home. Ms. Nelson had been hiding in the garage at the time of the murder, trying to obtain the blackmail photos Simon had of her, and accidentally set the house on fire while trying to destroy them. The fire gave her the opportunity to escape from Tad in the ensuing confusion.

After the apprehension of the drug gang, Max had talked to the county district attorney, explaining the details of Ms. Nelson's involvement. When hearing all the evidence from Max, the D.A. declined to press any charges against her.

"No trouble, I just told the D.A. the facts, and he couldn't see any reason to press charges. I assume you've told your boss and your fiancé?" Max asked.

"Yes, yes I did. Mr. Foley was very understanding. In fact, he gave me a new job as head of advertising and promotions. I did have a rocky time with my fiancé, Jim, for a while but in the end, he realized that I wasn't to blame and forgave me," Nelson explained.

This last statement of Ms. Nelson rubbed Max the wrong way, but she didn't say anything.

"So, you set the date and everything's okay?" Max questioned.

"Well yes, and no," Nelson said.

"No?" Max asked, puzzled.

"Well, we picked out our rings and we have the location set but I don't really have any women friends that I associate with since I moved to Royal Oaks," Nelson stated.

Max didn't like the way the conversation was going but asked anyway, "And?"

"And I was hoping that you might stand with me as my bridesmaid and witness at the wedding. You're the closest person I have as a friend here in Royal Oaks and I would really appreciate it if you could do it," Nelson pleaded.

"Oh, I don't know," Max responded, shaking her head in the negative.

"Please, please, please," Nelson pleaded.

Max thought for a moment, thinking about her life in Royal Oaks and how she had to deal with the workings of the male dominated society of the police department and politicians. She really hadn't had any time to make any female acquaintances either. This might be an opportunity to broaden her horizons. *Why not, what could it hurt?* she thought. "Okay. When and where?" Max replied.

A look of joy came over Ms. Nelson that Max found contagious. "Thank you so much. You have no idea how much I appreciate this. I'll send you the date and Mr. Foley has said we can have the wedding here."

"Here at the Renaissance fair?" Max asked.

"Yes, but also here at the chapel. You wouldn't mind wearing a costume, would you?" Nelson questioned. "Jim wants to have a medieval wedding."

Max began to immediately regret agreeing to the wedding. "Medieval?" Max asked.

"Actually Viking. Jim and his brother are members of the Society of Viking Research. We thought it would be really cool to have a theme wedding and hold it here," Nelson explained.

The images of scantily clad Viking women running around in bad Hollywood movies, popped into her mind. "I don't think so," she stated, bluntly.

Ms. Nelson immediately took out her cellphone from her pocket and pulled up a photograph that was on it. Showing the photo to Max, she saw a female model wearing an exquisite gown consisting of a white under tunic and a forest green over tunic that was covered with elaborate embroidery and bead work. On either shoulder was an oval brass brooch. The whole costume was fastened around the waist with a broad leather belt that wrapped abound twice and hung down to the knees.

Max had to admit that the dress was extremely attractive. "Very nice, "Max commented, "You'll look lovely in it."

"That's not the bridal dress, Chief Somers. That would be your dress if you say yes," Ms. Nelson pleaded.

Max thought for a couple of seconds. *The dress was extremely attractive. What do I have to lose? It might be fun and so, why not.*

"Okay, I'll do it on one condition," Max conceded.

"Yes," Ms. Nelson almost squealed with excitement. "Anything, anything you want."

"Can you find a spot for Mr. Randall? I would like him engaged in this endeavor too." Max asked with a wicked smile on her face.

"Certainly. No problem. We can fit him right in." Ms. Nelson expounded, giving Max a big hug for joy. "Consider it done."

After their conversation was over, they started walking to catch up with the others who were far in front of them. They caught up just as the group arrived at the front gate. Foley and Ms. Nelson excused themselves and headed back to the administration offices as Mr. Smith went to notify the limo driver that they would be leaving shortly. Lars Morgan shook Randall's and Max's hands and then walked off in the direction of the waiting limo, leaving Assumpta alone with the both of them.

"It has been a pleasure collaborating with you, Mr. Randall," she said, shaking his hand again. Then taking Max's hand with both of hers, Assumpta slipped a business card into Max's hand. "Very nice meeting you, Chief Somers. I hope we can talk again," she said. She then turned and walked away toward the waiting limo. After she left, Max examined the card Assumpta had placed in her hand, The front had the name, address, and telephone number of her law firm but on the back was a handwritten note with the words- 'Call me Please,' along with a telephone number that was different than the front of the card.

Randall saw Max examining the card and asked her, "What's that?

"An invitation, I guess?" she replied, slipping the card into her back jeans pocket.

Chapter 11

The next couple of weeks flew by quickly for Max. She had the mayor place advertisements in the Minneapolis newspapers, looking to interview for the two new police officer positions that the mayor had given her permission to hire. Max was amazed at the number of responses that the city had received.

The Royal Oak's human resources department had done the primary screening and sent the names of viable candidates to Max for her, to schedule interviews with. Max had wanted to hire candidates who had military backgrounds and law enforcement experience, In the end, there were three applicants, two women and one man that stood out above the rest. She ended up hiring the man and one of the two women, Katrina Jackson and Jeff Hall.

Max wasn't thrilled with not hiring both of the woman applicants, but she knew that she had hired the best applicants. In the end, she was happy that at least one of the new hires was a woman.

Toward the end of the week, she made the call to Ted Russell, the State Attorney General, and declined his invitation to endorse his re-election campaign, citing the mayor's advice to stay out of politics. He didn't take it well.

The following weeks seemed to fly by for Max. She soon realized that being the Chief of Police, even for a small town like Royal Oaks took up a lot of her time, what with training the new recruits, paperwork, and her everyday duties. It seemed that she was spending less and less time with Randall or maybe he was spending less with her. Either way, they were apart much more than Max liked. She kept hearing the little voice in her head telling her that she would just have to adjust to the new reality that went with her job.

The month of July appeared much faster than Max expected. About a week before Ms. Nelson's wedding day, a special delivery package notice was delivered to her apartment and the package was waiting for her at the apartment complex office when she got off work.

Opening it up, she saw it contained her Viking dress for the upcoming wedding. Trying it on, she looked in the mirror with approval at how it fit and looked. After putting it on a hanger and hanging it in her closet, she decided to call Randall. The phone rang a couple of times before he picked up.

"Hello, girlfriend," he started out. "How's life going?"

"Busy, boyfriend. How about you?" she replied.

"Same. Between Washington, the business, and dealing with Foley and the Morgan's at the Medieval fair, I'm stretched kind of thin. Oh, by the way, Assumpta keeps asking about when you'll call her back?" he responded.

Max kicked herself mentally, realizing she had neglected to return her call. "Tell her I'll talk to her this weekend, if it works with her schedule," she replied.

"I'm sure it will as she'll be at the wedding, too," he said.

Surprised, Max replied, "Really?

"Yah, it seems that Lars Morgan is a friend of the groom and his brother, and by the way- Thanks for dragging me into this wedding ceremony. I got my costume today and I am not amused," he complained.

"What are you wearing and what are you doing for the wedding?" Max questioned, laughing to herself.

"Some type of medieval pants, a tunic and a pair of furry boots that apparently ten rabbits gave their lives to cover them," he responded, "and I'm also an usher."

Max had a hard time not laughing out loud. "I'm sure you'll make a great usher," she commented and then added. "Do you want to go to the wedding together?"

"Love to. Seems like we haven't seen each other much lately and this will give us a chance to catch up. Pick you up about eleven?" he asked.

"Sounds good. I took the weekend off, so maybe we can do some more catching up at your place after the wedding?" Max queried.

"Great, and since you have the weekend off, maybe you can road trip with me Sunday," he replied.

"Sounds fun. Where are we going? Max questioned.

"Alexandria," Randall responded.

"Virginia?" Max asked, inquisitively.

"No silly, Minnesota," he shot back with a smile.

Chapter 12

The July wedding day broke sunny and warm. Randall was prompt in picking up Max at her apartment. She brought her suitcase with the bridesmaid dress and other incidentals she needed and threw it into the back seat of Randall's SUV. When they arrived at the Medieval fair site, they were ushered to the building being used as changing area for the wedding participants.

Ms. Nelson had helpers, make up people, and a hair stylist ready to transform Max into a Viking maiden. The makeup people did a touch up first, then the hairstylist braided Max's hair into two buns on the side of her head. Lastly, the helpers assisted her into her dress. After all was complete, Max looked at the full-length mirror placed in the room. She had to admit that the dress was beautiful.

"You look fantastic." Max heard a voice say behind her. "I hope I look as good as you do in my dress." Turning, she observed Assumpta Morgan standing in the doorway, looking at her with her dark penetrating eyes.

"Thank you," she responded. "John told me you would be here, but he failed to mention you were in the wedding too," Max replied.

"I don't think he knew. I'm kind of a last minute add on. You know how weddings start out small but seem to grow with a life of their own," Assumpta stated. Max nodded in agreement.

By this time, the assistants latched onto Assumpta and began doing the Viking transformation on her too. Max figured that this would be a good time to explain why she hadn't followed through with contacting her back.

Assumpta was more than understanding, as Max explained how busy she was getting settled back into her police chief position.

"I can understand your delay. Sometimes things just get in the way. You get so busy with life that you can lose your sight line." Assumpta said.

"Sight line? Max said inquiringly. "I'm not sure what that is."

Assumpta went on to explain, as the hair stylist started working on her. "In the old Irish culture, the concept of a sight line is especially important to some of the old folk. It seems that many Irish women often have what is called a second sight, the ability to see into the future but they cannot change that future, only see it. Some people today call it a premonition. But a few of these special women have what is called sight line vision or the string of destiny, the ability to see into the future and influence a change, based upon what they see in their dreams. In olden times, some people call them witches," Assumpta explained with a smile.

"And you have this sight line ability?" Max asked jokingly.

"Oh heavens no. My mother often told me that she had the second sight but unfortunately, she didn't pass down that ability to me. It's a shame though, because being a lawyer, such talent would be very beneficial in court. Don't you think?" Assumpta asked, with a sly smile.

"Yes, I guess so," Max responded, thinking that something in her voice didn't ring true.

"Look, I'm having a small get together next weekend. How about you and John stop in for a while and we can talk," Assumpta stated.

"Sure, I guess," Max replied hesitantly.

"Great, John has my address and I'll contact him about the date and time." Assumpta retorted, standing up to put her dress on.

"Okay, I guess I'll see you then," Max replied.

A few minutes later a person came and informed them that the wedding was ready to start. Max and Assumpta walked over to the wedding chapel that was festooned with flowers and decorations. Max was impressed with how much effort was made to make the chapel look truly medieval. Max notice that all the guests were also dressed in medieval garb.

She spotted Randall doing his ushering duties and gave him a wink as he spotted her. He gave her a wink back and then a thumbs up sign to let her know that she looked fantastic.

The wedding went off without a hitch and afterwards, the wedding party had the reception dinner. After the dinner, Max and Randall partook in a couple of dances, and stuck around for the cutting of the cake and the round of toasting the wedding couple, then excused themselves and headed back to Minneapolis and Randall's penthouse.

The next morning Randall and Max took off early in his SUV for Alexandria. Randall told Max that it would only take a couple of hours to get there if the weather cooperated. The weather didn't cooperate.

They ran into a torrential down pour a couple a minutes after leaving the penthouse which delayed them because of the heavy stop and go traffic. Finally, after getting in the northern suburb of Minneapolis the weather and the traffic cleared, and they started making good time. Reaching the city of Saint Cloud, they stopped for a quick breakfast at a restaurant along the highway. After getting back on the road, Max put her head on the side window and watched the scenery pass by. Looking out the side mirror to see how much traffic was behind them, Max noticed a black pickup with heavily tinted windows about a quarter of a mile behind them. It didn't really stand out to her, as it was just one vehicle out of many on the highway that day, but for some reason, it caught her attention. Thinking nothing of it, she went back to watching the scenery passing by.

It took about an hour for them to get from Saint Cloud to the center of Alexandria. Welcoming them at the downtown park, was a thirty-foot statue of a Viking warrior carrying a spear and a round shield. On the shield was written, 'Alexandria, birthplace of America.'

"Pretty impressive, don't you think?" Randall asked her, pointing to the statue.

Max remembered a statue of Texas hero Sam Houston that she had observed when she had driven between Houston and the prison in Huntsville that had to be at least twice as tall.

"Yes, very impressive," she lied convincingly.

"Here we are," Randall exclaimed, as he parked the SUV across the street from the statue.

"Here where?" Max questioned.

"The museum," Randall responded, pointing to a sign over a store front door. It read 'Runestone Museum.'

Getting out of the SUV, she and Randall proceeded to walk into the store. Max briefly observed display cases filled with artifacts, many local newspaper articles that were framed and hung on the walls and even a small dog which appeared to be sleeping on a rug in front of a log cabin facade. Walking over to pet the dog, she realized that it had died and had been preserved, and put on display, a long time before.

Randall smiled, seeing how Max had been fooled. He then went up to a woman who was behind the counter and introduced himself. The woman then called an elderly man out from another room in the museum. Max wandered around looking at the articles on the wall and the display cases, as Randall talked to the man. After a few minutes, Randall walked over to where Max was and handed her the keys to the SUV and asked her if she would go out and unlock it and open the back door of the vehicle. Max dutifully did what Randall asked. Standing by the open SUV door, she observed Randall and the other man carrying a large wooden crate and then sliding it into the back of the SUV. Randall then closed the door and taking the keys from Max, proceeded to lock the vehicle up. With that done he said, "Let's find some lunch."

Chapter 13

Sitting in the restaurant, Max's curiosity couldn't be contained any longer.

"Okay, what's in the box? she asked as they waited for the waitress to bring them their lunch.

"I don't know if I can tell you as its kind of a secret," he replied with a smile on his face.

"Come on, stop teasing me. Tell me, what's in the box?" Max pleaded.

Randall paused for a moment and then responded. "A rock. A two-hundred-pound rock."

"Stop kidding me," she pleaded. "What's really in the box?" Max asked again, getting frustrated with Randall.

"Really- it's a very large, heavy, special rock," Randall replied.

"Okay, what makes this rock so special?" Max queried, with sarcasm in her voice.

"Well," Randall paused as the waitress brought their lunch, "this rock has an awfully long history in Minnesota. It's so special that it has its own name."

"A rock with a name? Is this a takeoff on the old pet rock craze?" Max asked incredulously.

"Time for a little Minnesota history," he replied, pausing to take a bite of lunch. "Back around the turn of the century, a farmer near Kensington, Minnesota, found a rock in his field that had Viking runes carved on it."

"Wait, what is a rune?" Max asked.

"A rune is a medieval Viking alphabet symbol or letter. Many of the letters are like the modern, English alphabet but many are completely different," he explained. "This rock was supposedly found in the roots of a tree he was removing from his field."

"You said supposedly?" Max asked.

"A lot of experts investigated the rock after it was found and most concluded that it was fake, probably made by the farmer who found it." Randall continued, "Anyway- fake or real- many Minnesotans have taken the Viking story to heart. After all, they named their professional football team after them. And that my dear, is the brief history of the Kensington stone," he concluded, eating the last of his lunch.

"And that is what is in the box? The Kensington stone, right? Max questioned, finishing her lunch.

Randall paid the bill and continued, "Yup, Foley and the Morgan's had to buy a million-dollar insurance policy on it and make a whole bunch of promises to a lot of people in order to get permission to borrow the stone and put it on display at the fair. The stone will go on display in the Viking long house, locked in the plexiglass display that I designed and built.

"Now it all makes sense. Your display was especially designed to look like a rock, to house and protect a rock. A big rock," Max said kiddingly.

"Yup, and Foley and the Morgan's are risking a lot of money in advertisement and promotions to make this rock a profitable venture." Randall concluded, as they started to walk out to the SUV.

They then started heading back to Minneapolis. Randall told Max that they should be back home around dinner time. As they headed down the highway, they didn't notice the black pickup with heavily tinted windows that pulled out of the restaurant's parking lot behind them.

Chapter 14

The trip back to Minneapolis was uneventful. Max offered to drive a spell, but Randall said that he was good to make it all the way, so Max put her head on the side window and took a nap. She was asleep when Randall texted several of his employees and arranged to have them meet him at his office building. Max woke up just as they were arriving to the northern suburbs of Minneapolis. Randall informed her that they were going to make a stop before heading back to his penthouse.

"Why the stop?" Max asked.

"Going to deposit our cargo in the safe at the office," Randall replied.

"Why? Are you afraid that someone might steal your big rock?" Max asked kiddingly.

"Never can tell, but probably not. But I'm not going to take a chance. This rock has a million-dollar price tag on it. So, in the vault it goes until I can get it to Foley on Monday," Randall replied.

Finally arriving at the Randall Security building, Randall drove to the back where they were met by several men standing on the landing dock. Backing into the loading dock, Randall opened the back door of the SUV. The waiting men easily slid the wooden box out of the vehicle and carried into the building and into the cargo elevator. Taking the elevator up to the third floor, they carried it into, what appeared to Max, to be a bank vault door. Randall spun the dial on the door, turned the handle, and pulled the massive door open. The men then carried the box into the vault and carefully deposited it on the floor. Randall then closed the door and spun the lock mechanism to secure the vault door.

Thanking the men, he and Max headed to Randall's penthouse where they spent the remainder of the weekend.

Early Monday morning, Randall and Max took off to head back to Royal Oaks. Max had to get to her apartment and change into her uniform as she oversaw the day shift at the police station. Randall dropped her off at her apartment, gave her a kiss goodbye and headed out to the Medieval fair to inform Foley that the Kensington stone was safely under lock and key in his vault.

Max had planned this week for the training of the two new recruits. These new recruits were as different as night and day. One was an African American woman, fresh out of the army, after serving six years. She had a ten-year-old son and an ex-husband; the other newbie was a was a middle age ex-marine who had spent twenty years in the Corps and then retired.

Max thought that between Mark Wilson, her new deputy chief, and herself, they could evaluate the new recruits by having them ride along on patrol individually with each of them. After the second day of training, she and her deputy chief got together and compared notes about the new people.

Wilson was impressed with the overall ability of the ex-marine and how easily he took to fitting into the Royal Oaks police department, as was Max. The new female recruit was another matter. They both agreed that she was going to need additional time and training, after her orientation, but that she had a lot of potential.

After two days of working with the new recruits, she sent them to the Royal Oaks Human Resources department to fill out their final paperwork. Max decided to take the opportunity to catch up on her paperwork. After a while she decided to head out to the medieval fair and see if she could find either Ms. Nelson or Randall there.

Arriving, she was surprised at the amount of activity taking place. Workmen were completing many of the last minute details and vendors were moving into their new locations and setting up their wares for sale. Max found Ms. Nelson in her new office at the newly renovated admistration building. Max was impressed by the exterior of the building that was disquised to look medieval on the outside, but when she walked inside, the interior was as modern and up to date as any contemperary office building.

"Looks like you're getting close to opening with all this activity going on," Max opened with.

"Close, very close," Ms. Nelson replied. "We're having a soft opening next week. You will be coming , won't you?" she pleaded with a smile.

"Wouldn't miss it," Max smiled back. "You didn't happen to see John on site, did you?"

" As a matter of fact, I did. When I saw him this morning, he and several men were hauling a big box down to the long house," she replied to Max. " I can take you down there. I would like to see how his final set up of the display is looking."

It didn't take long as Ms. Nelson grabbed her walkie- talkie, and escorted Max to a golf cart waitng behind the administration building. On the drive down to the Viking village, Max asked her, " So, I was wondering, how come you kept your maiden name instead of your new husband's name?"

"Oh, I don't know. Jim didn't seem to mind that I kept my maiden name, and I think that Liz Nelson sounds better than Liz Linkmiester. Jim didn't seem to care one way or the other, so I kept it. And since we are going to be friends, you can just call me Liz instead of Ms. Nelson. Tell me, what would you like me to call you, Maxine, Max or Chief Somers?"

"Just call me Max. That would probably be best." Max replied.

About that time, they arrived at their destination. Max and Liz got out of the golf cart and walked into the Viking long house. The front doors were already open and because of the dim lighting, they could barely see the men working on the display at the other end of the building. Walking towards them, Max saw two men driving long bolts into the plexiglass and the concrete slab disguised as the center stone, on which rested a gray stone slab propped upright by a wooden stand.

"This must be the Kensignton stone," Max stated as they walked up to the work men. Randall turned around and smiled at Max, as the two women walked up to them. "Yes, this is the famous Kensington stone," he stated, proudly.

Max walked around the display, taking in the details of the stone. It stood about thirty inches tall and sixteen inches wide and was about 6 inches thick. It was a dull gray colored stone, with lettering carved into the flat upper surface. The lower part of the rock was gouged out and rough with no writing on it.

"What does it say, all this writing on it?" Max asked Randall.

" Well," Randall paused for a second. "If I have it correct, it tells about thirty northmen or Vikings, traveling from Vinland, and camping two days away from the stone. Twenty of them went fishing and when they came back, they found their commrades killed. On the side of the stone it says that ten men were guarding their ship, fourteen days away from the inland sea." Randall continued, "Vinland is what they called the Atlantic coast, and the inland sea probably Lake Superior."

" Sounds plausible to me. Why do they call it fake?" Max asked.

" Because some of the lettering is wrong," a voice asnswered back, coming up behind them. Max immediatly recognized the voice.

"Tom Edwards," Max said , turning to face the man walking out of the darkness. "What is the head Minneapolis medical examiner doing here?"

" That's head medical examiner and medieval geek," he replied with a smile. Max proceeded to introduced him to Randall.

" What do you mean the lettering is wrong?" Max asked after the introduction.

"Well, back after the Kensington stone was found, many experts examined it and based upon the style of runes carved into it, determined that they were too modern to have been carved during the age of the Vikings but now things have changed," he stated.

"Changed? How?" Randall asked.

" The early experts based their assumptions on archeological information availabe at the time they examined it. Since then, new archeological research has started to contradict ealier findings and more and more of that research has found that runes found on the Kensington stone do match the new information," Edwards informed them.

"So it's real?" Randall asked.

"Maybe- the jury is still out on it." Edwards replied. "More time and more research is needed, but in the end, I'm pretty sure it will be validated." He continued as he walked up to the display. " This certainly is an attractive setting for it, I must say."

"Thank you," Randall responded, feeling pride in his accomplishment.

"What brings you here, today?" Max asked.

"Day off, and I heard a rumor about the display from some of my fellow members in the SVR. Thought I'd get an early view" Edwards replied.

"You're a member of the Socity for Viking Research?" Max asked.

"Yes I am," he answered. "Along with my wife and my two boys. I've been a menber for about ten years but my wife joined before I did. The boys love the LARPing side of the society. When we're participating at events, they really appreciate that they don't have to wash their hands before a meal."

" What's LARPing?" Max asked. "I've never heard that term before."

"LARPimg stands for live action role playing. Members take on a personna of a person who would have lived in that time frame and try to recreate as accuratly as possible that person, based upon historical research. There are many LARP groups, Civil War, World War I or II, Western, and in our group- Viking. Seems that just about every culture or time period has a LARP group," Edwards continued.

"Really- never heard of such a thing," Max exclaimed.

" But you participated in one," Liz piped up.

It took Max a moment to think. Then it dawned on her. "The wedding?" Max asked.

"Yes-The weddng," Liz replied. "Both my husband and his brother are members of the society and now, so am I."

"You'd be surprised as how many people belong to our group," Edwards lectured. "We have many professional people, doctors, lawyers, politicians, teachers, plumbers, and.."

"Medical examiners," Max interjected.

"Yes- even medical examiners," Edwards replied with a smile.

Chapter 15

Max woke up Saturday morning to the sound of rain hitting her apartment patio awning. Max loved the sound of the rain in the morning. It was so relaxing that she just laid in bed and listened to it fall, almost falling asleep again and wishing Randall was there to enjoy it with her. But he wasn't. He had gotten a call from Washington the day before and left on a private jet for a meeting with his superiors in D.C.

Randall told her he would be back either Monday or Tuesday, and that she would have to attend Assumpta's party alone. This did not thrill Max at all. Realizing that she couldn't get out of it, she dragged herself out of bed and started the day.

That afternoon, she pulled up to Assumpta's address. The house was in an exclusive section of Minneapolis that was part of a gated community. Giving her name to the security guard at the gate, she quickly gained access and drove up to the address that Randall had given her.

The house was huge, with tall Greek pillars in the front, and a massive circular driveway that surrounded a Greek revival fountain. Parked in the driveway were several expensive sports cars and a couple of limousines. Max felt very self-conscious, parking her sedan amongst all the other cars.

Walking up to the front door, she thought, *What the hell am I doing here?* Steeling her nerves and taking a deep breath, she rang the doorbell, half expecting a butler with a day coat and white gloves on, to answer it. Instead, she got Assumpta.

"Welcome Chief Somers," Assumpta said, as she looked past Max. "John didn't come with you?"

"No, he was called out of town suddenly," Max explained.

"Well then, that gives us more girl time together. Doesn't it?" Assumpta replied, taking Max by the arm, and ushering her into the house. As they walked through the huge entry way, Max was struck by the opulence of the interior. The house looked like something out of a magazine with high cathedral ceilings and massive woodwork covering the walls and trim.

As if reading Max's mind, she told her, "Inheritance from my late father. He owned several taconite mines and several shipping companies north of Duluth, up on the iron range. He bought this place as a residence for when he was in Minneapolis on business. When he passed on, I inherited it," Assumpta clarified, as she led Max through the living room. As they were walking, she looked through the outside glass wall of the living room, at the massive indoor swimming pool, with about a dozen people in swimming suits, partying.

Assumpta led her into a room off the main living room, what appeared to be a library or den, with leather furniture and floor to ceiling bookcases, mostly which appeared to be law books.

"My condolences for your loss," Max offered to her.

"Thank you, but it's been almost fifteen years since they died," Assumpta explained as she offered an over-stuffed leather couch to her.

"They?" Max asked, as she sat on the couch, impressed with how comfortable it was.

"My father and Lars's mother. A private plane crash on the way up to Duluth. Very tragic," Assumpta stated in a matter-of-fact way, not trying to display her emotions.

"Before the trip, I had a dream about the crash. When I told my father about it, he just brushed it off as a girlish dream. I wish he would have listened to me, but he didn't," she continued. Max let the enormity of her statement sink in.

"And your mother? Is she still alive?" Max asked curiously.

"No, she died when I was eleven," Assumpta said. For the first time, Max saw Assumpta's dark eyes water, as emotion came over her face.

"Sorry. Too personal?" Max asked, regretting asking the question.

Assumpta quickly dried her eyes on the sleeve of her blouse and then sat on a leather chair across from her.

"This isn't a party, is it?" Max said curiously. "At least not for me."

"Very astute Chief Somers, and you're right, this really is Lars' party," she said, gaining her composure. "I needed an excuse to meet with you. That's why I gave you my card at the fair. I'd offer you a drink, but I know you don't drink alcohol. What is it now? Eight years with AA? Perhaps you'd prefer a soda?" Assumpta asked, getting up from the chair to obtain one for her.

Max indicated to her that she was fine. Assumpta sat back down as Max asked her, "What else do you know about me?" As she started to feel very uncomfortable with the way the conversation was going.

"Oh, I have a whole dossier on you. High school dropout, got your GED, joined the military, two tours in Afghanistan, two marriages, widowed once, divorced once, a daughter in college in California and you suffer from PTSD," Assumpta stated.

Max just sat there, letting the enormity of what Assumpta had said, sink in. She felt her face turn red as anger started to swell in her.

Assumpta, seeing her reaction, jumped up from the chair and sat down next to Max. "Don't be angry. I'll explain everything," she said. "The truth be told; I admire and respect you very much. You see, all my life, I've been handed everything I wanted. Everything came easy for me, from wealth to my law degree. I'm what you could call an entitled bitch. I know it and can accept it.

"But I just want you to know how much I admire how you've scratched and clawed your way to where you are, just like you scratched and clawed your way out of that grave Tad Paulson put you in. You're strong and you're a fighter. I told you before that we need strong women in politics. I had you vetted because I need you to work with me."

Max let the enormity of what Assumpta said, sink in. After a few moments and regaining her composer, she asked, "What do you mean 'work with you?' You know I turned down Ted Russell's offer because I don't want to get involved with politics. Why should I do it for you?"

"Because after I'm elected as the State Attorney General, and I will be elected, I want you to be the first woman to head the Minnesota State Police," Assumpta stated, looking straight into Max's eyes.

Max sat silent, letting what Assumpta had said register in her brain. She could feel a presence, almost a power of dominance, emanating from Assumpta's dark gaze.

Assumpta broke the silence, "Look, go home. Talk to John about it. I know he loves you very much and would give you the best advice. He'll do you right. Trust him. He's a good man and has your best interest at heart."

Max let what Assumpta said sink in and replied with a smile, "Yes, he is a good man."

"I was told that he wanted to marry you and you turned him down. Is that right?" Assumpta asked with a smile.

"Now how would you know that?" Max asked incredulously.

"Because I lured him here a couple of times under the pretense of working on his project. You know he is a nice-looking man and to tell the truth, I kind of fancied him. But all he would ever do is talk about was his fair project and you, and I quickly realized that I didn't have a chance with him. So, if you don't want him, let some of us other girls have a swing at him." Assumpta exclaimed, taking Max's hand, and smiling devilishly.

Max, starting to smile back said, "Keep your hands off him, friend. He's mine."

"Are we friends?" Assumpta asked warmly.

"I guess we are, for now. But if you touch John Randall, I might have to arrest you, or worse. Understood?" Max said, giving her a pretend stern look.

"Understood," was Assumpta's reply. "But please consider my offer. Minnesota needs you and I need you. You'd be a great asset to my administration.

As Assumpta escorted Max to the front door, she thought to herself. *I really should hate this woman, but instead, I think I really like her.*

Chapter 16

Max got home from her meeting with Assumpta late in the afternoon and since she was working the night shift on the weekend, she fixed something to eat, changed into her uniform and drove to the police station. After a quiet night on duty, she went back to her apartment, fixed some breakfast, and then went to bed.

It didn't seem like she had been asleep very long before she realized that Randall was there in bed with her.

He must have gotten back from Washington, she thought as she felt Randall's hands start to explore her body. He covered her with kisses all over, as she started to feel the heat of passion starting to build.

A stray beam of afternoon sunlight found a crack in the closed blinds covering Max's bedroom window and struck her in the eye, causing her to wake up, alone. Looking around the room, she realized that Randall had only been a dream. A dream she had thoroughly enjoyed, but a dream none the less. She wondered why she had that specific dream at that specific time. She figured that it must have been the conversation she had with Assumpta on Saturday about dreams and the sightline.

At least this was a pleasant dream instead of like the ones she had last year, where she dreamt, she was drowning. That dream, however, did come true when Tad Paulson's henchmen tried to torture her by immersing her in a large vat of water. She thought it funny though, that she never had that dream again after it became reality. *Hopefully, this last dream will come true when Randall gets back from Washington*, she thought to herself with a smile.

That night Max was on night duty again, and again, in the morning, Max closed the bedroom window blinds, taking particular attention to cover them with a sheet, so as not to have any interruptions by the sun if she had another pleasant dream about Randall. She then tried to fall asleep.

Again, Randall came to her in her dream, but unlike the last dream, she dreamt she kept her eyes closed, only feeling what he was doing to her but not watching. When Randall stopped, she couldn't stand it anymore. In her dream, she saw herself opening her eyes and seeing Randall, not as the man he was, but that of a corpse lying beside her in the bed, wrapped in bandages that were stained with blood.

The shock of her vision caused her to sit up in bed, wide awake. *My God, that seemed real,* she thought to herself. It prompted her to grab her cellphone sitting on her nightstand and text Randall, asking if he was all right and when he would be back. It took thirty excruciating minutes before he replied on the phone, that he was fine and that he would be back the following day. He then sent an emoji of a heart and she replied by sending one back.

Still shaken, and with the phone in her hand, she decided to text Assumpta that she needed to see her. Her phone rang back almost immediately.

"Made up your mind already?" Assumpta asked.

"No, I just need to see you. I need to talk to you," Max responded.

"I'm in the limo on the way to the medieval fair. I could stop at your place on the way, if you like," Assumpta stated.

"That would be great," Max replied, with a quiver in her voice.

"You sound shaken. Are you alright?" Assumpta inquired, concern sounding in her voice.

"Yes, I'm fine. I just need to talk to you about something," Max said hesitantly.

"About?" Assumpta asked.

"Dreams," was all Max said.

It took twenty minutes for Assumpta to arrive at Max's apartment. Knocking on the door, Max let her in.

"Nice place," Assumpta stated as she came in, looked around and then sat down on the couch.

"Says the woman who lives in a mansion," Max retorted with a smile.

"It is said that home is where the heart is, and I can tell your home is here. Now, what's so important that you had to talk to me about dreams. Do you mean your dream about being the head of the state police?" she asked with a smile.

Max shook her head no, then proceeded to tell her about her drowning dream and it eventually becoming reality and then continuing on, told her of her most recent dream about Randall. After telling her all the details, Assumpta sat silent of a couple of moments, letting everything sink in what Max had told her, and then suddenly blurted out, "I need a drink."

"I have nothing here for you," Max answered back.

"I know, so come with me," as she took Max's hand and led her out of the apartment and to her limo. Her driver saw them coming and proceeded to open the back door for them as they approached. Once inside the limo, Assumpta opened a portable bar installed in the driver seat backrest. Handing a soft drink to Max, she then poured herself two fingers of what appeared to be whiskey out of a glass decanter and drank it down. Raising up her empty glass, she asked Max. "Sure you don't want one?"

"No, thanks, I have one," Max told her, holding up her soft drink.

Assumpta again poured a second drink, but this time only finished about half of it.

"Listen, I know exactly how you feel. When I was twelve, like I told you, I had a dream about my parents dying in a plane crash. After I had the dream, I begged my dad not to fly up to Duluth. He was supposed to go alone but Lars' mother, my stepmother, decided at the last minute to accompany him," Assumpta told her, finishing off the rest of her drink.

"That's when their plane crashed. Right?" Max stated.

"Right," Assumpta confirmed. "Ever since then, I am a firm believer in prophetic dreams. That's how I know that I'm going to be elected Attorney General."

"You dreamt it?" Max asked.

"Yes, I dreamt it, and I also put a lot of money into my campaign, and I trust the polls."

"But what about my dream about John? Is that going to become reality?" Max questioned.

Assumpta thought silently for a few moments and then said, "Remember at the wedding, we talked about second sight and the sight line? I think you've got one of the two. Hell, maybe both," she stated, finishing her drink.

"I guess that means you do to, and if you do, that means you lied to me about not having it." Max stated.

Assumpta replied to her with a sly smile, "One of the first things you learn as a politician, is how to lie."

Chapter 17

Randall was scheduled to arrive home the next day from Washington, late. Since Max was working the late shift again, there was no way to be able to welcome him home, so she waited until the next afternoon to call him. She was in a quandary as to telling him about the dream or not. She finally figured it would be best to wait until she saw him in person, as she was quite sure that he would dismiss it as silly.

Arriving home from work that morning, she saw a message on her answering machine. Not recognizing the number, she automatically hit the play back button. Attorney General Ted Russell was on the other end of the phone message.

"My sources tell me you're thinking about endorsing Assumpta Morgan in the upcoming election," the message started in an accusatory manner.

"I thought you said that you were staying out of politics, and I took you at your word. You better think long and hard about endorsing her, because if you do, I can make your life very, very miserable. Let me repeat- don't do it," was the message left on her answering machine.

Max was confused by the content and viciousness of the message. She hit the save button on the message, hoping to replay it for Randall after he got back.

Maybe I will have Randall talk to his people in Washington and have them yank his chain, she thought to herself.

She decided to drive into Minneapolis the following day and see Randall. Calling to tell him of her decision, he replied by telling her that he had to go out to the medieval fair for some last-minute adjustments on his Kensington stone exhibit. Hearing that, she changed her plan. He asked what would be best for her: meet her at the exhibit, or at her apartment? Max asked him to meet at her apartment after he was done at the fair.

Later that afternoon, Randall showed up at her place looking tired and exhausted. Max ushered him in and then proceeded to smother him with kisses.

"Wow, with a reception like that, I'm going to have to leave town more often. Do you want me to stay overnight with you?" he asked her with a grin.

"It would be wonderful but I'm working the late shift and I only have about an hour before I'm on duty." Max replied.

"How long do you need to get dressed and get to work?" he asked coyly.

"I've done it in less than a half an hour before," Max replied with a smile, getting his drift.

"We can get a lot done in thirty minutes," he replied with a smile.

He was right.

The next morning, Max got off duty and returned to her apartment. The place smelled of Randall's aftershave he kept in her medicine cabinet. She surmised that he must have spent the night there, as the bed had been remade and there were wet towels in the bathroom from where he must have taken a shower that morning. *Damn, I wish he had stayed until I got back.* She thought to herself. *Oh well, I'm too tired to do much, even if he was here,* fondly remembering their encounter the previous afternoon.

Grabbing a piece of toast and some orange juice for breakfast, she turned down the blankets on the bed and the closed the blinds in the bedroom, she laid in her bed, thinking about Randall. She didn't want to fall asleep for fear of having the nightmare again, but her exhaustion caught up with her and she did eventually go to sleep.

Waking up later in the early afternoon, she was relieved that her dream hadn't re-occurred. She decided that she wouldn't tell Randall about her nightmare, writing it off as just a silly dream she had because she had missed him so much. *If it occurred again, I'll talk with him about it,* she decided.

Finally, the weekend came, and with it the end of her night shift duties. Saturday was the soft opening of the Medieval fair and she had promised Randall that she would make an appearance. When she got there, the parking lot was almost full of vehicles.

Surprisingly good turnout for the first day, she thought, finding a place to park, and walking up to the gates. It was a nice warm late-August day.

Randall had been hired several years ago by the fair management to oversee the overall security at the fair. Max remembered that this was where she had first met him over a year ago.

As she walked to the gate with her ticket, she saw his security crew dressed in their colorful Swiss guard uniforms, taking the tickets, and ushering the crowd in through the gates. She recognized a couple of her own officers, moonlighting for Randall, while off duty. Walking up to one of them, she handed him her ticket and smiled at him. He recognized her and said to her,

"Welcome Chief. Have great day," smiling at her, and taking her ticket.

"You too, Johnson. Looking good," she replied, adding, "Do you know where John Randall is?"

"Last I heard, he was down at the Viking village," he replied.

"Thanks," she said, as she started walking through the front gate.

As she walked through into the fair, she observed the crowd as they shopped at the different vendors, who were selling their wares from their stalls. She also observed many other people walking around with roasted turkey legs and other edible treats.

Jugglers, musicians, and entertainers pleased the crowds that were gathered around watching them and busking for any money that people provided. It was a beautiful fall day, that everyone seemed to be enjoying.

Approaching the Viking village, she saw Viking costumed people standing on the palisade, welcoming the visitors to the new addition of the medieval fair. Walking through the wooden gates, she saw the crowds were heading to the Viking longhouse, so she joined the que. Once inside, it was obvious that some of the crowd was enjoying the displays of the merchants, but most of the people were gathered around two men dressed in heavy leather amor, and metal helmets that were fighting each other with swords and shields. They put up a very convincing performance as the struck at each other convincingly until the larger man was tripped by the small, more agile warrior. Sprawled on the ground, the larger Viking warrior signaled that he yielded to the smaller man. The winner then reached down to the man on the ground and extended his hand to help his defeated enemy up off the ground.

The crowd applauded its approval and began to disperse. As the two warriors began to remove their helmets, Max recognized the winner. It was Tom Edwards, the medical examiner. Walking up to him, Max clapped her hands, showing her approval. Edwards looked up and smiling at Max stated to her, "Greetings Chief. I guess you caught the battle?"

"Yes, I did. It looked very authentic. Was it choreographed?" she asked.

"Wish it was, then I wouldn't hurt so much. Even blunted swords can do damage," he stated as he showed her a red welt starting to form on his arm, where he had been hit by his opponent.

"Can I ask a stupid question? Max asked.

As if reading her mind, "Because it's fun, good exercise and I meet a lot of good people." He responded as he took off more of his armor.

"Okay, I guess you get asked that a lot," Max responded sheepishly.

"Yeah, I do. But that's alright. I always enjoy talking about my hobby. But you already know that don't you?" he stated, taking a long drink from a bottle of water, and removing the sweat from his face with a towel that he took from a canvas bag located on the ground.

"Sure do, but I have another question. Have you seen Randall anywhere?" she asked.

Pointing to the other end of the longhouse he told her, "Last time I saw him, he was down by his display, but that was an hour or so. Not sure if he's still there."

Max thanked him and headed over to Randall's Kensington stone display. There were a line of people waiting to get close to the stone. Max was impressed about how many people were showing an interest in an old stone with writing on it. Finally getting closer to the display, she saw Randall and Lars Morgan standing off to the side, talking. Lars was first to spot Max and told Randall, who then came over to where she was standing, and asked her to join them.

Walking over to where Lars was waiting, she looked at Randall's display. Each of the four columns had a man dressed in Viking armor and animal skins, holding a spear and a round shield, guarding the display. There was dim lighting on the columns and a bright spotlight centered on the Kensington stone, drawing visual attention on to the stone. A recording explaining the stone's history and a translation of the writing on it was playing in the background from concealed speakers. Max was impressed.

Chapter 18

"Aren't your guards a little overkill?" Max asked Randall with a smile.

"Window dressing," Randall replied. "The SVR is providing volunteers for the display. In return, they get a sizable donation to their group finances."

"Well, they really look convincing, and your display seems to be a hit," she said as she watched the line of people waiting to see the Kensington stone stretch farther down the Viking longhouse.

"I'm glad that my part is over. Now I can get back to my real job here. Hey, are you hungry?" Randall asked Max.

"Sure, what have you got in mind?" Max questioned.

"Ever had a fried turkey leg?" Randall asked back.

"No, I can honestly say I've never had a turkey leg," Max replied.

"Then you're in for a real treat. What about a hot apple dumpling with ice cream?" Randall replied, taking Max's hand, and leading her to the food court.

Later that night, Madge, the Royal Oaks police dispatcher called Max at a little after two in the morning, informing her of a disturbance at the Medieval fair and that emergency vehicles had been dispatched.

It only took a few minutes to get into her squad car, and hitting the siren and strobe lights, she made it to the Medieval fair, arriving about the same time as the ambulances.

On the way to the site, she took one of her PTSD medication pills dry, having nothing to wash it down with.

One of Randall's fair security people met them at the service gate and directed them to the Viking longhouse, telling them to hurry, as there were several casualties. Max wondered, as she got out of her squad car and ran to the longhouse, what kind of accident might have happened? Getting closer to the building, she saw a huge gaping hole where a wall had been at the far end of the building, a whisp of smoke from it rising into the cool, late August air. Entering the longhouse, she observed people around Randall's display. Max saw two people were laying on the ground being tended to by emergency medical personnel, and a third person lying under one of the four pillars that had been toppled on its side. Two men were trying, without results, to lift the pillar up to free the trapped man underneath it.

Quickly, Max and the emergency people with her, pitched in together and slowly began to lift the fallen pillar off the victim. Max grabbed the unconscious man's legs and slowly slid him out from under his concrete prison.

"Careful Chief, he may have internal injuries," one of the emergency personnel yelled at her.

"I've got him clear," she responded to the others.

The men dropped the pillar and at once started examining the freed man for injuries. When they turned him over, Max realized who the man was all covered in blood. It was John Randall.

Chapter 19

"John? John, can you hear me, John?" Max cried out, kneeling over his body. He quietly moaned. His eyes closed.

One of the medical personnel attending to Randall ordered her to stand aside as they put a cervical collar around his neck. Another person started an IV drip in his arm and a third placed an ambu bag over his mouth and nose and started squeezing it intermittently.

She heard someone say, "He's lost a lot of blood. I think we're losing him."

"No!" Max screamed aloud. Panic in her voice.

"Get out of the way officer, and let us do our job," one of the emergency personnel told her as he bent over and placed his fingers on Randall's neck, searching for a pulse. "Get one of the ambulances down here, stat. Tell them to come through the employee entrance. We need them here and now," he shouted at her.

Max hesitated for a moment, then got on her radio and sent the message to the waiting ambulances. She then changed the radio frequency and contacted the Royal Oaks police dispatch and told them to send additional people to assist her at the site.

"What's his name?" the head medical person asked her.

"Randall- John Randall," Max replied.

Just then an ambulance drove through a side gate near to the long house. Its siren blaring.

As they loaded him into the waiting ambulance, the medical person asked, "John- John Randall. Can you hear me?"

Max saw no response. Again. the medical person asked, "John- can you hear me?" Again, no response. He then used his thumb to raise the closed eye lid of Randall. "Hurry," was all he said.

Just as they were starting to close the ambulance door, Max saw the medical technician inject Randall with a syringe straight into Randall's heart. Closing the door, the ambulance and the medical people tending Randall were gone. Siren and lights piercing into the night. Max stood there listening as the sound of the wailing ambulance slowly disappearing into the darkness of the night.

Standing there, in the dim light of the Viking longhouse, she felt so all alone. Then suddenly snapping out of her fugue, she realized there was still activity going on around her. Looking around she realized there were still other medical people there and two other bodies, lying on the ground. Walking over to one of the other medical people, she asked quietly, "What about the other two people who were injured?"

The person replied, "Sorry officer, they didn't make it."

Max stood silent for a moment, letting it sink into her brain, and then asked, "How?"

Picking up a piece of plastic shrapnel from the ground, and showing it to her, the medical person replied, "Cut to pieces from flying plastic or from an explosion, or both. They didn't stand a chance. They bled out almost immediately. The third guy must have been standing behind the pillar when the explosion went off."

Max then started looking around at the scene. Shards of thick plastic Lucite were scattered everywhere, covering the ground, one of the four pillars were broken off, and the other three pillars bent at angles, and the Kensington stone was gone.

This was a robbery? What? For a damn stone? Was it worth the lives of these men? she thought to herself.

Max's first instinct was to follow the ambulance to the Royal Oaks hospital, but her common sense kicked in and instead, she started looking around to try and figure out what had happened at the site. As she began to secure the scene, she saw, through the blown-out hole in the wall of the long house, two of her officers walking through the employee entrance. *Thank God, some help,* she thought to herself. Then she recognized who the two officers were. They were deputies Jackson and Hall, her two rookies.

Still grateful for the help, she shouted for them to start securing the scene. "No one comes in here unless they're authorized. We have two fatalities and one serious injury, and this is our crime scene. Get your gloves on and start looking for anything that might be a clue to what happened here. Follow protocol and record everything."

"Jackson, I want you to get ahold of Tom Edwards, the Harris County medical examiner. Only talk to Edwards. Get him out of bed and out here fast. Got it?"

"Hall, I want you to figure out how someone could remove a two-hundred-pound rock out of here," she barked out.

"A two-hundred-pound rock? Did I hear you correctly, Chief?" Officer Hall asked.

"Yes, you heard correctly, and Jackson, after you get Edwards on the phone, call the station and get some more help out here. I want every available officer here as soon as possible," Max dictated as she started to head toward her vehicle.

"Where are you going, Chief?" Officer Jackson asked.

"Hospital," she replied. "I need to interview our surviving witness," she explained to them, as she started leaving the longhouse.

Getting to her squad car, she turned on her siren and strobe lights as she sped off toward the Royal Oaks hospital. Arriving there, she ran to the front desk at the emergency entrance, and asked the nurse behind the desk, as to where Randall was being treated. The nurse directed Max to the third floor. Foregoing the elevator, Max took the stairs, two steps at a time. Arriving at the third-floor nursing station out of breath, she asked again for John Randall. The nurse seemed to take forever to find the information on John.

"Let me page his doctor," the nurse stated after locating his room on her computer.

Max heard the hospital speaker softly page Doctor Manville to the nursing desk. Max had a sinking feeling in her stomach, as she impatiently waited for the doctor to respond. *Why does that doctor's name sound familiar?* Max thought to herself. When he finally came to the desk, she knew why. He was the same doctor who treated her the year before.

"Hello Officer Somers. You're here for John Randall, aren't you?" he said in a matter of fact, emotionless, tone of voice.

"Yes, I am. Can I see him?" she asked.

"You can see him, but you can't talk to him," the doctor replied.

"Why not?" Max asked. Almost afraid to ask.

"Mr. Randall came in here more dead than alive. He's lost a lot of blood, sustained a couple of broken ribs, has a punctured lung, a concussion and swelling of the brain. After putting two pints of blood in him, we had to hook him onto a ventilator to keep him breathing and put him into a medically induced coma until the swelling in his brain goes down. He's not going to be speaking for a while," the doctor explained.

Max felt like somebody punched her in the stomach. "I see," was all she could say.

"I can notify you if his condition changes, one way or another," the doctor continued.

"What do you mean, one way or another?" Max questioned. "He is going to make it, isn't he?"

"It can go one way or another. We'll know better in a few days. In the meantime, he's getting around the clock care. If there is any change, we can contact you. Okay? Do you want to see him now?" the doctor asked.

"Yes, please," was all Max could say.

The doctor escorted her into a glassed off emergency room. She could barely recognize Randall, with all the cables, tubes, and bandages, which covered him. Her dream about him became all too real.

Oh John, what did you get yourself into? she thought to herself.

Seeing a nurse standing next to him on one side of the bed, Max walked over to the bed on the other side, and lightly touched his hand, tears starting to well in her eyes. The nurse, seeing Max's tears, handed her a Kleenex, and asked, "Husband?" Max shook her head in the negative. The nurse asked no more questions.

As Max dried her tears, her mind was racing over all about what had happened in just a few short hours after that wonderful afternoon at the Medieval fair.

Trying to control her emotions, she made a silent vow to find out what occurred and bring to justice whoever did this.

The nurse asked if she wanted to be notified if there was any change. Max gave her a business card and told her yes. Max then asked the nurse if Randall's clothes he was wearing when he was brought in were available. The nurse went over to a cabinet and pulled out a large, sealed plastic bag that held Randall's clothing, shoes, and wristwatch. Max thanked her, then clutching the bag walked over to Randall, touched his motionless hand, and then left the room, not knowing if she would ever see him again.

Chapter 20

Max left the hospital, got into her squad car, then had started crying again. The possibility of losing Randall was almost more than she could stand. She had gone through the heart break of losing someone she loved twice before. She found it difficult to go through it again. Finally, wiping away the tears, she steeled herself to finding out what happened to him.

Driving back to the Medieval fair, she ran through her mind what possible scenarios could have brought Randall out to the site in the middle of the night. Arriving at the employee entrance at dawn, she saw six of her officers on the scene, all processing the remains of the explosion. Officer Jackson was the first to see her arrive. Walking up to Max, she started giving her an update, "The Medical Examiner should be here in about twenty minutes, Chief, and I got four other officers to help process the crime scene. I also think that Officer Hall has some information you'll want to hear.

Looking around, she saw Officer Hall heading in her direction, carrying something in his hands.

"Chief, I think I got something important here," he said, setting the objects on the ground.

"What have you got?" she asked.

"Well, the ambulance pretty much destroyed any tire prints coming through the employee's entrance, but I did find some tire tracks just outside the entrance. I made plaster casts of them, matching the treads to both coming in and going out," pointing to the objects on the ground. "I also found some paint scrapings on one side of the entrance," holding up a small plastic bag with a substance in it. "I then measured the width of the tire tracts and checked online to see what vehicles match that width," he concluded.

"And?" Max asked.

"I concluded that since just about any car or pickup could make it through the gate easily, the only vehicles that might have trouble making it through might be an ambulance or our mystery vehicle. Since the paint doesn't match any ambulance paint colors, it only leaves one other vehicle." Officer Hall explained.

"Which is?" Max asked, growing irritated.

"A Hummer," Officer Hall stated. "And I'll bet if the tire treads are measured from the plaster castings, we'll find the departing treads are deeper than the arriving treads, proving your two-hundred-pound rock was on that vehicle when it left."

Max was impressed. "Good work, both of you," then telling officer Hall, "So we got a Hummer and its color. Get the paint scrapings to forensics and find out what color it is and the year the paint was used, then I..." Officer Hall interrupted her mid-sentence, "Midnight blue and probably painted when it was new in 2018."

"And how do you know that?" Max asked.

"The internet. It's got all the answers," Officer Hall stated, holding up his cell phone.

"The internet? Well, just to be sure, I want forensics to confirm it too. So, get it to them and when they do confirm it, I want you to alert all the Hummer dealerships and body shops in a two-hundred-mile radius, to be watching for a Hummer, a 2018, midnight blue Hummer with scratches on its side panel. Got it?" Max ordered.

"Yes sir," he replied, as he ran off to fulfill Max's orders.

"What do you have for me, Officer Jackson?" Max asked, turning her attention to her other officer.

"Well not as much as officer Hall, but you might find this interesting," she said, holding up a piece of what appeared to be a piece of cotton padding.

"What is it? Max asked.

"Somebody tried to use a shaped charge using cotton padding on the Lucite, but they used way too much explosive. And unless I am wrong, from the smell of the explosion site, I think they used two different types of explosives, nitroglycerine on the Lucite, and dynamite on the wall of the exhibit," she explained. "I think we have two different people setting the charges, each one familiar with different types of explosive devices. One setting the nitro, and one setting the dynamite. I also believe, based on the body positions and wounds, that all of the victims might have been involved with the explosion."

"Explain," Max demanded.

"Well, both victims took the Lucite explosion on the front of their bodies and were blown away from the blast, as if they were in close vicinity to the explosion. The third victim was shielded behind the concrete pillar, but because of the excessive amount of explosive, he was

trapped by the falling pillar," she explained.

Max thought for a second, digesting all the information she had been given. "So, you think that the two dead bodies set the explosions and were killed through their own incompetence? Then the third party was accidently injured, trying to shield himself, knowing the explosion was going to happen? Is that what you're saying?" she questioned.

"That would be my best guess, Sir, or he was just lucky," Officer Jackson replied.

This information caused Max to pause for a moment or two. She then asked Jackson,

"Where did you learn all this explosive stuff? The internet too?"

"No ma'am. Eighteen months in Ordinance Division at Fort Lee, Virginia," Jackson replied. Max was impressed with her credentials.

"Well okay then. Let's follow the evidence. I want you to get explosion trace off our two fatalities' clothing. I have the clothing of our survivor in my car. Search through the clothes, and then tell me if the evidence follows your supposition. The stuff in my car hasn't been entered into the chain of custody, so I want you to do a thorough search, particularly for a cell phone, and enter everything and anything you find. Got it?" Max ordered, handing her the keys to her vehicle.

"Yes sir," Jackson replied, and then started to head off to follow her instructions.

"When it's all collected and accessed, get it to the Medical Examiner, okay?" she ordered.

"One last thing, Officer Jackson. Don't call me ma'am."

"Will do, Chief," Jackson replied, as she walked away.

Standing there in the longhouse, Max couldn't help but reflect on how far police work had progressed, with the internet, military training, and forensic science. But even more importantly, she couldn't figure out why Randall had been at the medieval fair in the middle of the night.

Chapter 21

Tom Edwards, the Hennepin County medical examiner along with several other men from the medical examiner's office, arrived on scene shortly after Max had sent her two rookie officers on their tasks. Finding Max, Tom let her know that he was on site. Max requested his help in trying to identify the two dead bodies. Tom stated that he had his finger printing kit and that he could run their prints for identification. As they walked over to the first of the victims, she filled him in on what she knew and what she wanted. She told him that the fingerprints of the victims and any trace residue from the clothing would be needed and that the clothing from a third victim would be in his possession when he got back to his office.

Arriving at the first body, Tom bent over to examine the face. Rising suddenly, he hurriedly moved over to the second body and examined it too. Turning to Max, he exclaimed, "We don't need fingerprints, I know who these men are. They're members of the SVR. This one is Stan Newgate and the other is Ron Sorenson."

"What?" Max exclaimed. "Why would two members of your society be involved with the explosion and theft of a rock?"

"I have no idea," he responded, "but I'll sure as hell try to find out."

He then signaled for the other men he arrived with, to bring the gurneys they had set up over to the scene. With speed found with years of experience, Tom's team quickly placed the bodies in body bags and had them transported to the waiting vehicles.

Tom pulled Max over to the side as the bodies were being prepared for transport and whispered to her, "You know that I'm not going to be able to personally help you with this case. Right?"

"Because you know them? Yes, I figured that out when you said you knew their identities. Conflict of interest. Am I right?" Max stated quietly.

"True. But that doesn't mean I can't help you in other ways. I'll do what I can to keep you in the loop. Okay?" he replied softly.

"Sounds good to me, but just to give you a heads up, I should let you know that our third victim in the hospital is John Randall," Max whispered back to him.

"John Randall? Your boyfriend, John Randall?" Edwards responded, surprised. "How's he doing?"

"Yes, my boyfriend, and he's in serious condition. But he's a fighter, and when he can talk, he should be able to tell us what went on here," Max told him confidently, not betraying her fears that it might not turn out the way she hoped for.

"Wow, I guess we both have a conflict of interest," he replied, then adding, "look, I'll keep you informed with what I find, and maybe you can help me on my end. Deal?"

All Max could respond with was one word. "Deal." They then shook hands and went their different ways.

Max spent the next three days between the hospital and the police department. The gossip about Randall's injury had already filtered through the building. Mark Wilson, her Deputy Chief, told her that he was willing to fill in for her as much as possible, if it would help her out. She thanked him and then kiddingly told him that he just wanted more overtime because he had a new baby on the way.

"You're right about the overtime, Chief. But it's also about getting out of the house. The wife is driving me crazy as she's in her last trimester. By the way, you're going to get a baby shower invitation in the mail soon. The wife said she would understand if you can't make it, what with Mr. Randall being in the hospital and all," he explained.

"Tell her that I'll be there, short of some kind of major disaster," Max promised.

That afternoon she headed to the hospital to check on Randall. Arriving there she was informed that John had been moved from the emergency room to an ICU room. Max felt that that was a good sign. Arriving at Randall's floor, she checked in at the nursing station and was informed that there was a one visitor limit allowed in his room, and there was already someone in there. Puzzled as to who the visitor was, she took a seat in the reception area, to keep an eye on his door and to wait her turn.

After ten minutes, she saw the door to Randall's room open. Max was surprised at who walked out. It was the man who saved her from Tad Paulson, Mark Richards. He was heavier and had a full beard, but it was him.

"Mark, Mark Richards, where have you been?" Max asked as he almost walked past her on the way to the elevator.

Surprised by Max's exclamation, Mark stopped and recognized Max. "Chief Somers, so good to see you. John didn't tell you?"

"He didn't tell me what? You just disappeared after you saved my ass, a year ago," Max stated trying to keep her voice down.

"John thought it would be best for me to get out of Minneapolis for a while, so he sent me to San Antonio to set up a branch office there for Randall Security. Got married to Cindy, and was doing some investigative field work, when I heard about Randall being injured, so I hotfooted it here to see if I could help," Mark explained.

"Cindy? John's secretary, Cindy?" Max questioned.

"Yup, that Cindy. So, maybe you can fill me in on what happened?" Mark asked her, looking at Randall's door.

He continued, "The nurse explained that they stabilized him, but he's still in an induced coma. Kind of short on details as to what happened. Maybe you can catch me up?" he asked her.

"Glad to, but this is not the place. I'm going to check in on him first, and maybe we could talk down in the hospital cafeteria? The coffee isn't too bad," Max stated.

"Sure. I'll meet you down there in a couple of minutes. Is that okay?" Max questioned.

"Sounds good. You still drink your coffee black?" Mark asked.

"Yup." Max replied, as she started walking into Randall's room.

After about twenty minutes, she joined Mark in the hospital cafeteria. Her coffee was waiting for her. Sitting at the table with Mark, at an out of the way table, she started the conversation. "Well?"

"How are you holding up?" he asked her.

"Holding up just fine," she lied, taking a sip of coffee. "But before we discuss John, I have some old business to discuss with you."

"Old business?" Mark questioned.

"Yes. First, I need to thank you for saving my life," Max paused, "And ask you a question."

"You're welcome," Mark replied, and then asked, "And your question?'

"Was it self-defense?" she asked, taking another sip of coffee.

"You mean Paulson?" Mark questioned.

"Yes, I mean Paulson. Was it self-defense?" she repeated.

Mark paused for a second or two, before responding, "Yes, it was self-defense. Paulson had drawn his weapon and was going to take you out when I gave him another target, other than you. He aimed for me, and I put him down."

"Good enough for me," Max replied with a sigh of relief, "Look- I need your help figuring out why John was at the medieval fair well after midnight, and what really went down there. You're my miracle man, and John and I need you," Max continued.

"Shouldn't there be video on the CCTV that he installed? I saw the plans for the exhibit. John had at least four cameras set up. And as for the proximity alarms, they should have been able to signal any activity around the exhibit. Why didn't they work?" Mark questioned.

"I don't know, I'll check it out, but maybe this might help," she stated as she looked around to make sure that no one was watching, then reached into her pocket, and removed a cell phone, covered it with a napkin and slowly slid it over to Mark on top of the table.

Mark took the napkin and cellphone and stealthily took it off the table and put it in his pocket.

"John's?" he asked, knowing full well what the answer was.

Max nodded her head in the affirmative, and then quietly stated. "I've got officers looking for it now, so I need it back soon. I don't want anything deleted or changed. I just want a heads up on what's on it. You know that I officially can't be involved in the investigation, but I need to know why he was at the exhibit so late at night. Will you help me?"

"Of course, I will," Mark responded, "How much time do I have?"

"I figure twelve hours or less, before I will have to find it. Understand?" Max stated.

"Okay. I'll need a few hours to figure John's password and do a download of his info. I'll get it back to you as soon as I'm done," he told her.

Max nodded her head, drank the last of her coffee, and gave Mark a hug. He hugged her back. The two of them then headed out of the hospital to their cars.

Max decided to head back to the fair and check with Ms. Nelson about the security camera footage that Mark had asked about. Arriving at the fairgrounds, she headed to the administration building hoping she could find anything that might give her some answers. She found Ms. Nelson waiting for her in the front office. Curious as to how Ms. Nelson knew Max was coming to see her, Ms. Nelson took Max to a room in the back of the building. Upon entering, she observed a long console in the middle of the darkened room and a wall that contained multiple television screens mounted onto it.

"As you can see, Mr. Randall has every square inch of the grounds covered with cameras. I just happened to be in here when I saw you pull into the parking lot," Ms. Nelson explained.

Max was both impressed and hopeful that the security footage might give some clues as to what had happened the night of the break in.

"Is everything recorded?" she asked hopefully.

"Yes, most of it is, but you're not going to like what you see," Ms. Nelson stated as she walked over to the technician sitting at the console.

It took the technician a minute or two, pushing several buttons before the main screen started projecting images the camera that had covered the exhibit, came up. Max observed Randall's exhibit, dark and empty of people for a couple of minutes before she saw a couple of shadowy men come into view. Both figures wore balaclavas that covered their faces. One carried a backpack, while the other one looked right into the camera and made a slicing motion across his throat.

Immediately the screen went blank. Max looked at Ms. Nelson and asked, "Is that it? There isn't anything else?"

"No, I'm sorry," Ms. Nelson replied.

"What happened to all the cameras? Surely they must have been more than that? Where's the security alarms?" Max asked.

"Tell her, Tim," Ms. Nelson instructed the technician.

"I ran a diagnostic on the system, and it seems that someone hacked into the security system and shut it down. They had access to the camera feeds and turned them off when the intruder made the hand signal, that you saw there," he explained. "I tried to track the intrusion back, but I hit a firewall that I can't break through it."

"Nothing?" Max questioned.

"Sorry, but nothing," he replied.

Max was stunned and aggravated. "Damn it. Why is this stupid rock worth all this effort?" she exploded. Calming herself down, she asked Ms. Nelson, "Can I get a copy of this tape sent to me?"

"Of course. I'll have Tim send it to your office. Will that work?" Ms. Nelson replied, as the two of them walked out of the security room. Once the security room door closed, Max asked. "What do you know about Tim? Could he be involved?"

"I doubt it. He doesn't work for us. He's one of Randall Security's people. He had been here during the whole installation of the system. I don't think Mr. Randall would let him monitor the system if he didn't trust him, do you?" she replied.

"Aside from him, who else would have access to the security system?" Max asked.

"Just the Randall Security people. Even our employees don't have access to it," she responded.

Max shrugged her shoulders and. countered, "Okay, I guess that answers all my questions. By the way, you know that I was never here, right?"

Ms. Nelson silently shook her head yes. Max thanked her and headed to her car but felt very uneasy. Something felt wrong, very wrong about the whole situation.

Chapter 22

By the time she got back to her office at the police station, there were two emails on her computer, waiting for her. One contained the footage of the security camera that she had asked for from Ms. Nelson, and the other was a message from Mark Richards stating that he found what he was looking for and that they should meet where they met last. Max understood what he meant, so she quickly made a copy of the video footage on a flash drive and headed over to the hospital cafeteria. Arriving before him, she waited outside the hospital for a couple of minutes until she saw him walking through the parking lot. She let him pass her by and then walked into the hospital foyer, following him in. Mark made a side trip to the men's rest room, leaving Max to enter the cafeteria alone. The only other person in there was a cafeteria worker behind the counter. Going up to the counter, she ordered two coffees and took them to the table where she and Mark had sat before. She quickly placed a paper napkin over the flash drive that was resting on her lap.

When Mark came into the cafeteria, he spotted her, and headed over to where Max was sitting and sat in the chair opposite of her.

"Any good news?" she asked.

"I don't know," Mark replied. "His password was your birthday. You'd think someone who owned a security company would have a more secure password."

"He was always a romantic," Max quipped.

"Anyway, nothing out of the ordinary was on his phone. Photos mostly of his projects, and of you. But his call log was a little puzzling. Most of his calls were work related or conversations with you, except for his last one," Mark explained.

"What do you mean?" Max asked.

"Here, read this," he stated, sliding a sheet of paper across the table to Max.

Max picked up the piece of paper and read it. Her blood ran cold. All it said was 'Meet me at the exhibit tonight, 'A.'

"Look at the phone number and the time stamp," Mark pointed out to her, "Eleven fifteen at night."

Max looked at the message again. She recognized the phone number and there was only one person who had an initial that fit the message. *Assumpta. That bitch*, she thought to herself.

"You're sure about this?" she questioned.

Mark shook his head in affirmation. "Yup, but I'm not done going through the source of the message. There are a couple of anomalies in the source codes that I need to investigate some more," Mark explained.

Max didn't understand anything that Mark said but still asked, "Do you need the phone longer?"

"No, I don't. I made a clone of his phone, so I can do everything I need to do on it," he stated.

"What do you mean by a clone?" she asked.

"An exact copy of his phone downloaded into a similar phone. I don't need the original as I can work with the copy," he explained.

Max shook her as if she understood, but she really didn't. "Okay, as long as you're working on the clone thingy, maybe you could look at this?" she said, as she slid the napkin- covered flash drive across the table to Mark.

Clandestinely taking the napkin and flash drive and putting the flash drive in his pocket, he asked, "What is it?"

"It's the video of the break-in at the fair. At least up to the point when someone turned off the cameras and alarms. Maybe there is something you can glean off it," Max stated finishing her coffee and taking the napkin off the table and putting it into her pocket.

Mark then stood up from the table, downed the rest of his coffee and said, "I'll do my best, but this isn't looking too good for John, is it?"

No, I fear not good. But one way or another, we have to figure out what went down there. Right?" Max asked.

"Right," Mark replied, and then left, leaving Max still sitting at the table, contemplating the whole situation. She knew the first thing she would have to do was figure out a way to get Randall's phone into evidence. She then needed to talk with Tom Edwards, and she knew for certain she was going to have a long talk with Assumpta Morgan. *I need to know what the hell was going on. Was Assumpta responsible for John being on site just as the stone was being stolen, and how was the SVR related to the theft?* she thought to herself.

Leaving the hospital cafeteria, she went to her squad car in the hospital parking lot. Sitting in the car and using the napkin that the phone was wrapped in, she proceeded to wipe the phone off of any fingerprints. She placed the cellphone in an evidence bag and sealed it.

She then returned to the police station and found her deputy chief, Mark Wilson, in the parking lot. Pulling him aside, she took Randall's phone and handed it to him. She told him that she had located it under some debris at the crime scene and wanted to make sure it got into the evidence locker.

"Am I going to find anything on it?" Wilson asked her.

"I don't know. I sealed it without looking," she lied.

Wilson looked at her in a knowing way, like he knew she was lying to him. After a moment or two, he put the phone in his pocket and told her, "If you find any more evidence, make sure you call me or another officer before you retrieve it. Okay? You know you can't be involved in this. Right?" he stated, waiting for her confirmation.

"Right. You're the boss on this investigation. If I accidently find any more evidence, I promise to call you immediately. By the way, you might want to check out the security tape from the site," she said with a smile as she started walking into the police station.

He smiled back at her, "I will. We don't want any complications on this investigation, do we?"

"No sir, we sure don't," Max replied.

Chapter 23

When her shift was over, Max headed back to her apartment. After fixing herself some supper, she sat down on the couch and started writing down on a note pad all the information that had been uncovered. She them proceeded to write down how she could help in the investigation without violating her conflict-of-interest issue. The first item on her list was to investigate why Assumpta Morgan had lured Randall out to the Medieval Fair in the middle of the night.

As she was finishing up her list, she noticed that she had a text message from earlier in the day. The message was from Mayor Price, asking her to stop in and see him as soon as possible. She decided to see him the next day before she confronted Assumpta. She watched the evening news and weather on her television. The September weather forecast was for much milder temperatures than normal, but she perked up her interest when the reporter on TV broke the story about the theft of the Kensington stone and the death and injury of three people.

"If anyone has any information on the theft of the Kensington stone or of the explosion and death of the two men, please contact Crime Stoppers. There is a five-thousand-dollar reward offered for information leading to the arrest and conviction of those responsible," the announcer reported.

This isn't going to help anything now that everyone knows about it, she thought to herself. *All the crooks and crazies will be calling.* She was right.

The next morning Max went to the city hall to face the mayor. Arriving at his office, his secretary ushered her in to his office immediately.

Mayor Price thanked her for getting to him so promptly. "What's going on?" Max asked, knowing full well what the topic of discussion would be.

"This fiasco at the fair, is what's going on. But first, I want to give you condolences on Mr. Randall's injury. I understand that the two of you are close, right?" the mayor asked. Max shook her head affirmatively and thanked him for his concern.

The mayor then continued. "I've got messages from the State Police and the State Attorney General's office, offering to help in the investigation. Do we need help, Chief Somers?"

"No Sir. My Deputy Chief is handling the case, and so far, we're pretty sure of the type of vehicle that was involved and the type of explosives used. He also will be evaluating security video tape evidence from the scene. With confirmation from forensics, I'm sure he will be close to figuring out who's responsible for this crime." Max explained to him, confidently, knowing full well it wasn't anywhere near the truth.

"Good, but I want him to keep me updated about the investigation. Okay? The last thing I want to deal with is Ted Russell poking his fat nose into our business," the mayor responded.

Max took the mayor's last statement as a dismissal and left his office. Going over to the police station, she found Mark before shift change and asked him to stick around for a couple of minutes after work and meet with him in her office.

After the shift change, he walked into Max's office and asked, "What's up?"

"The mayor's up. That's what up. He wants an update of any information you find," Max explained.

"Why?" he asked.

"Because he's the mayor, and it seems he's trying to keep the State Attorney General out of our business. I guaranteed him that you have everything under control. Do you want the AG taking over here?" Max replied, growing irritated over the possibility of such a move.

"No Sir, I do not." her Deputy Chief responded.

"Good. Keep him in the loop as best you can. Okay?" Max asked.

"Will do, boss." he replied.

"Good. Go home and get some rest and enjoy the family," Max told him.

"Thanks, but the wife is getting miserable, and you know what they say about misery loves company," he countered.

"Get out of here," she ordered with a smile.

At lunch time she told dispatch that she was taking a break for a couple of hours and if they needed her for anything, contact her on the radio. She then headed into Minneapolis, to Assumpta's house. *This was not going to be pleasant,* she thought.

Arriving at the mansion, she rang the door and waited for someone to answer. It took a minute or two before Lars opened the door.

"Good afternoon, Chief Somers. How can I help you?" he asked pleasantly.

"Is Assumpta home?" she asked.

"Yes, she's in her office. Follow me," he told her.

As they walked to Assumpta's office, Lars extended his condolences to her about Randall and asked about his condition. Max thanked him and told him that Randall was stable and that was all she said about him. Entering Assumpta's office, Max found her sitting behind her desk on her cellphone. Raising her finger and then pointing at a chair, she continued her conversation. Max sat in the indicated chair and waited for her to finish her conversation.

Finally finishing, she asked Max, "Well, I'm glad to see you but I thought you'd be at the hospital with John. How is he doing?"

Max tried to stifle her anger and replied, "He's stabilized and holding his own, no thanks to you."

Assumpta was taken aback by the answer, turning red in the face, and then asked, "Why? What do you mean by that?" clearly agitated.

Max took out the paper with the text message that Mark had given to her and threw it across the desk. "Explain that," pointing to the paper. Assumpta picked up the sheet of paper, read it and then turned red.

"I can't," she stammered.

"Why not?" Max demanded.

"Because I never sent it," she replied.

Chapter 24

"What do you mean, you never sent it?" Max asked incredulously.

"Just that. Lars, and I, along with about fifteen contributors to my campaign, were at a fund raiser the night of the robbery, until almost one in the morning. I have plenty of witnesses that can confirm that. Besides, the dress that I was wearing had no room for a cellphone," Assumpta replied.

"Could Lars have sent it?" Max questioned

"I doubt it," she replied. "He was sitting by my side the whole evening."

"Well then, who? Where was your phone during this fundraiser?" Max asked.

Assumpta took a deep breath and replied, "Both my phone and Lars' phone were locked in the limo. We both agreed that we wouldn't carry our phones during our fund raisers. We didn't want to be disturbed by any incoming calls."

"What about your chauffer? Could he have used it or given it to somebody?" Max questioned.

Assumpta thought for a moment, "I doubt it. Charles has been with the family for as long as I've been alive, maybe longer. My Dad hired him years ago, and I trust my life with him. Besides, what would be his motive?"

Max thought about it and realized that she was right. *What would be his motive?* she thought to herself.

"What about Mr. Smith?" Max questioned.

"Nope, not with us," Assumpta bluntly stated. "And is no longer in our employ."

Getting out her cell phone, she called Mark Richard at Randall Security. "Mark, I'm with Assumpta Morgan, and she claimed the phone call didn't come from her phone. She says she can prove it, and I believe her."

Silence was on the other end of the phone, and then Mark replied, "Listen, give her my number and have her leave me a message. I have an idea. Give me fifteen minutes after she does that, then call me back. Okay?"

Max gave Mark's number to Assumpta and asked her to call it and leave a text message. They had waited for about ten minutes, when Max's phone rang. Answering it, she was surprised that it was Mark calling back so soon.

"She's not lying. She didn't send the message," Mark exclaimed.

"How do you know?" Max asked, incredulously.

"The source code is different. The phone message on John's phone came from a different phone than the one she just used," he explained.

"What?" Max responded. "How can that happen?"

"Remember when I told you I was going to clone John's phone? Well, someone did the same to the phone that Assumpta is using. Her phone has been copied and hacked.

I guess that puts us right back from where we started," he explained.

"Yes, I guess you're right," she said dejectedly. After pausing for a minute to ponder the implications, she responded, "Thanks Mark. I'll get back to you later."

Turning to Assumpta, she told her, "I have to inform you that your phone has been cloned and hacked, and, also to say that I am very sorry for accusing you. Can you forgive me?"

Assumpta stopped dead in her tracks, realizing the implications of what it meant to have a copy of her phone being used by somebody else, and all her personal calls and information being open for public use. She felt anger, worried, and violated all at the same time.

Assumpta hurriedly walked over to the office door, opened it, and yelled at the top of her lungs, "Lars, get in here."

After a few moments, he appeared at the door, and asked, "What's up, Sis?"

"My phones been hacked," Assumpta stated, almost in tears.

Lars stared at Assumpta's phone in disbelief and stammered, "Who? Why?" Then turning to Assumpta, asked. "Do you know when?"

"It had to be before the theft and explosion at the exhibit site," Max replied.

Lars then asked Assumpta, "Do you know what information was on your phone? Is there anything that could hurt the campaign?"

Assumpta thought for a few moments, "No, I don't think so. You have all the campaign info on your phone, don't you?"

"Yes, I do," Lars replied. "But what if my phone has been hacked too? Shouldn't we have both of them checked out?"

Max suggested that they might want to get all their phones checked. Lars said he would call Randall Security first thing,

"Ask for Mark Richards." Max suggested.

After Lars left to make the call, Max and Assumpta were alone in the room. Assumpta walked over to a paneled wall. "I need a drink," she said, pushing on the paneling. The panel revolved one hundred- and eighty-degrees, revealing a bar on the other side. Pouring herself a whiskey from a decanter, she took a long drink from the glass. Then looking at Max, stated, "I'd offer you one, but I know you'd refuse, and I don't have any soft drinks here."

"That's okay. I'm good. But more importantly, are we good?" Max questioned.

Assumpta walked over to Max, giving her a hug, stated, "We're more than good. We're friends. Good or bad, we're still friends."

Chapter 25

It was almost a week later when Max heard from Assumpta. She had come into the police department early so she could conference with her deputy chief and to check her phone for any texts that she might have received over night. One of the texts she received on her phone asked her to call back as soon as possible. Max didn't recognize the number in the text, but it was signed by Assumpta. Max called the number and almost immediately got Assumpta on the phone. She explained to Max that Mark Richards had done a complete diagnostic on her phone and Lars's too. He found that Assumpta's cell phone was the only one that had been compromised.

"I gave the old cell phone to Mark Richards to play with and replaced it with a new one with a new number, so please use this number to contact me," Assumpta requested, and then continued, "Anything new on John's condition?"

"Yes and no. The doctor said that his body is slowly healing but the swelling in his head wasn't going down, so they are still keeping him in a drug induced coma," Max stated.

"Don't worry. John is a fighter, and he's going to be just fine. You'll see. Do you need anything?" Assumpta asked.

"No, I'm good, just tired," Max replied.

"I'm sure you are. Look- if you need some down time, you're always welcome here." Assumpta offered.

"Thanks, but I need to figure out who put him in the hospital first," she countered,

"Okay, but if you change your mind, let me know. I'll talk to you later," she concluded.

"I sure will, and thanks for the offer," Max said as she shut off her phone.

Max proceeded to wait for the officers on her day shift to arrive. Mark Wilson, her deputy chief, was out answering a call so Max managed the shift change, roll call, and duty assignments herself. Finally showing up, he came into Max's office, threw his hat on her desk, and collapsed in the chair in front of her desk.

"Rough night?" Max asked.

"Sure was. It seems like every traffic stop on the highway needs a supervisor these days. Speaking of which, any chance of promoting a couple of officers to sergeant, so I can spend more time on my deputy chief duties?" he asked.

Max thought about it and responded, "Good idea. I've been so busy with other things, I guess it never crossed my mind. I'll run it past the mayor and get his approval. On personnel matters, how are the rookies doing?"

Mark thought for a second or two and replied, "Great, they both seem to be fitting in nicely. I think they're ready to hit the streets on their own. By the way, forensic reports came back, and our rookies were spot on in their evaluation of the evidence on the Medieval exhibit. The vehicle used was a Hummer, and the explosives were nitro and dynamite. Guess the kids did good."

"Sounds like it," Max stated then continued. "Any luck on locating the Hummer? How about the background checks on our two victims? Did anything turn up on them?"

Mark responded, "We sent out a text to all the Hummer dealers and body shops in the state, to be on the lookout for it, but so far, no luck. Our victims were both ex-Military. Both unmarried. One had a girlfriend, and the other was recently divorced and probably had a girlfriend. One was a used car salesman and the other was a plumber. It seems the only thing they had in common was they were both members of the Society for Viking Research."

"What about Hummer owners. Can we get a list of all the Hummer owners that bought a blue, 2018 vehicle?"

"Already done. Believe it or not, there are over thirty-five Hummers of that same year and color, owned in the state. I have Jackson running down the list of the owners now. I think she's about half done, but so far, nothing," Mark concluded.

"Well, I guess you got everything under control," Max responded. "You'll keep me updated on the investigation, right?"

"Right, boss," Mark responded. "It would be helpful if we could talk to Mr. Randall. How is he doing?"

"About the same. He's healing but still unconscious. And you're right, it would be nice to talk to him," Max replied, then as an afterthought asked, "did you run a check on our two victim's bank accounts?"

Mark thought for a second, "No, I didn't think of that. But I will," he replied.

"Good," Max said. "You'll keep me updated, right?"

"Right. And you'll talk to the mayor soon? Mark questioned.

"This afternoon," Max promised.

Max kept her word. She scheduled an afternoon meeting with Mayor Price and went over to the town hall at the appointed time. Entering the mayor's office, she sat down in the chair in front of his desk.

"How can I help you today, Chief?" he asked Max, as he shuffled some papers on his desk.

She asked him about the possibility of promoting a couple of her deputies to police sergeant to alleviate the pressures on her and her deputy chief. He promised to take the proposal to the city council when they next met.

The mayor then asked Max if there was anything else she wanted to talk about. Max sat quiet for a moment or two and then replied, "No," then after another pause, "well, yes."

"What's on your mind, Chief?" the mayor asked. giving her his full attention.

"Look mayor, this whole thing with the Medieval Fair and the explosion and theft, and my conflict of interest, has me feeling so helpless and useless. There's got to be a way for me to get back on the case. I seem to be directing it from the station but what I really need is to get more involved in solving it. The department doesn't have a detective on the squad since I'm the only one certified for that job, and I can't get involved because of this damn conflict of interest crap. There's got to be something we can do?" Max pleaded.

The mayor was slow to respond as he was deep in thought about how to answer Max's plea.

"Do you want me to call in the State Police to take over? If I do, you know the attorney general will be involved? Is that what you want?" he replied.

"No. God no. Not that," Max shot back.

"Then there's not much else I can do. You know Chief, that I was a lawyer before I was Mayor, and as a lawyer, I can tell you there's not much else you can do, except for resigning your office and becoming a private citizen," he paused. "And besides, I'm not going to accept your resignation any way," And then pausing again, "Unless?"

"Unless what?" Max questioned, seeing a glimmer of hope.

"Unless you have another deputy with you at all times when you are working on the case. That deputy would then record everything as far as the evidence you find, and you would not be able to do any investigation without that deputy next to you," the mayor explained.

"A babysitter?" Max questioned,

"A babysitter," the mayor confirmed.

"I'll do it," Max replied, joyfully, realizing that she could now get fully involved in the investigation.

"Why don't you get one of your new whiz kids, I've been hearing about lately. It would be good field training for them," the mayor suggested.

"Good idea, mayor. Thank you, sir, I'll do just that," Max responded as she left his office.

Chapter 26

Max returned to the police department after her meeting with the mayor. She informed her deputy chief about her meeting with the mayor, and that she would be pulling one or both rookies out of the rotation so they could babysit her.

"How do you feel about that?" Deputy Wilson asked.

"I'm okay with it. I guess we better inform our rookies that they're going to get a change of duty. Where are they now?" Max questioned.

"Officer Hall is off and officer Jackson is still running the search on the Hummer owners," he stated.

"Let's go give her the good news," Max said kiddingly.

They both went into the squad room, where they found Jackson at a desk just getting off the phone.

"Sirs, I think I might have a lead on the Hummer," she told them excitedly.

"What have you got?" Mark questioned.

"I just got off the phone with a Mr. Jack Taylor, who verified he has a Hummer that matched the one we're looking for. He said he had purchased it for his girlfriend recently, and that they had both flown down to Mexico and had been at his condo for the last three weeks. They had just gotten back to Bemidji yesterday, and that was when they realized that it had been in an accident while they were gone," Officer Jackson explained.

If he was out of the country for three weeks and just got back, that means he was in Mexico for a week before the explosion. Max thought.

As she was talking, Mark jumped onto a nearby computer and started doing a search.

"I found him," Mark exclaimed, "Jack Taylor owns a shipping company out of Bemidji and has his own airline. He even owns his own airport in Playa Del Carmen, Mexico, and is ranked in the top ten per cent of the richest men in the state."

"Where is Bemidji?" Max asked.

"About four hours north of Royal Oaks," Mark told her.

"Officer Jackson," Max ordered. "I need you to call Mr. Taylor back and make an appointment to interview him for tomorrow afternoon and tell him not to touch or do anything to the Hummer until we get there."

"We, Chief?" Jackson asked.

"Yes, we. You and I are going on a road trip tomorrow," Max explained to her.

Very early the next morning, Max and officer Jackson left for Bemidji. As they were driving along, Max asked officer Jackson to get on her phone and search the internet to find out who oversaw the police in Bemidji. After a few minutes of searching, Jackson informed Max that the Chief of Police's name was a person by the name of Sam Cooke. Max then instructed her to call the Bemidji police department and inform them that they were coming to investigate a case, and that any help would be gratefully appreciated.

Officer Jackson made the call. After hanging up the phone, she told Max that the Police Chief would be waiting for them at the Bemidji municipal airport, and that the full name of the Chief of Police was Samantha Cooke.

Samantha Cooke? Looks like I'm not the only female Chief of Police in the state, Max thought to herself.

Arriving in Bemidji a little after twelve, Max followed the directions to the airport that Jackson provided from her phone. Pulling up to the gated delivery entrance, they were met by a guard that asked for their ID's. Providing them, he ushered them through the gate after giving them directions to Jack Taylor's airplane hangar.

It didn't take long for them to find the hanger. Standing outside of it was a small, middle-aged, grey-haired woman, wearing a police uniform. Parking their squad car, the woman walked over to them. Max and Jackson got out of their car as she approached them.

"Chief Somers?" the woman asked, extending her hand.

"Chief Cooke? I'm so glad to meet you," Max replied, taking her hand, and shaking it.

"How can I help you?" Chief Cooke asked.

Max explained her situation, and Chief Cooke listened attentively. After Max had finished, Chief Cooke told her that she had two of her officers already inside the hanger where the Hummer was parked, as she ushered Max and Jackson through a doorway into the hanger.

It didn't take Max but a moment to see the Hummer and the two officers and a civilian standing beside the vehicle they were looking for. Chief Cooke introduced the two officers and the civilian to Max. The civilian turned out to be Jack Taylor, the owner of the Hummer and of the airplane hangar.

Taylor was a stocky, mid sixty, deeply tanned man, with a bad toupee. He had on a pair of khaki shorts about two sizes too small for him and a Polynesian style shirt that was half unbuttoned and reveled a heavy gold link necklace around his neck. With his Rolex watch and several heavy gold nugget rings, he made a silent statement- that he had money.

Max took an instant dislike for the man, although it was very unlike her to form an instant opinion of someone at first glance, she did so with him. He explained to the officers that he bought the Hummer for his girlfriend to use, and that same day, he had flown them both to Playa Del Carmen for a three-week stay at his condo. He explained that he had parked the Hummer in the hanger so it would be available to them when they got back. Upon arrival, his girlfriend noticed the dent and scratch on the driver's side door. He was at a loss as to how it happened as it hadn't moved during the time they were gone.

"You took the keys with you? Any cameras?" Max asked.

"No, I hung the keys on the keyboard in my office, and no, there are no cameras." Taylor stated, pointing to an office door on the side of the hanger.

"So, anyone could just walk in and grab the keys, take the Hummer, and return it, without you being none the wiser?" Max asked.

"Well, I guess so," Taylor replied. "But why go to all that work just for a joy ride?"

"Maybe to commit a crime with it," Max commented sarcastically.

Chief Cooke realized that Max was starting to lose her temper, so she quickly interjected. "Mr. Taylor, let us examine the Hummer, while you go and get us a list of all the people who would have had access to the keys."

"Okay, I guess I could do that," Taylor responded and walked off to get the information.

"Thank you," Max said to Chief Cooke. "Can we get started on the Hummer?"

"Sure thing. Did you bring a processing kit?" she asked.

"Yes, we did," Max replied. She then instructed Officer Jackson to retrieve the processing kits out of the squad car. When she returned to the hangar, Max, Jackson, and the two other deputies, started processing the Hummer while Chief Cooke walked into the hangar office to check and see how Mr. Taylor was doing. They finished the processing about the same time that Taylor and Chief Cooke walked up to them.

Handing her the paper with the information Max requested, she asked, "Done?"

"All done. And found a few things, but it was pretty well cleaned up by someone," Max responded.

Taking the paper, Max thanked her for all her help. Jackson and the two deputies placed a half a dozen sealed evidence bags in the processing kit. Then Jackson closed the kit and returned it to the trunk of the squad car.

"Can I take you guys out for lunch?" Chief Cooke offered.

Max thanked her but declined, saying that they would get a bite on the road on the way home. She then thanked her again for all her assistance.

"If you every need anything, just let me know," Max stated, shaking Chief Cooke's hand.

"The same to you. Us girls have to stick together, right?" Chief Cooke replied.

"Hey! Does that mean you're done with my car?" Taylor piped up.

Chief Cooke discreetly signaled Max that she would respond, "Yes, we're done. But in the future, keep your keys somewhere other than on a board in an unlocked office," she tersely replied.

Chapter 27

The trip back to Royal Oaks was a quiet one. Max let Jackson drive so as to give her a chance to catch some sleep as she was on the night shift rotation for the next week. She called her deputy chief to inform him that they might be a little late, depending on the traffic. After the call, it didn't take her long to drift off to sleep. She had the dream again, about Randall being dead. The dream caused her to spring wide awake when they were about twenty minutes from Royal Oaks. She looked at her watch, and questioned Jackson, "You must not have hit any traffic? Looks like you made pretty good time."

"Yeah, it's pretty light. You were sleeping good, so I tried to make it as smooth as possible. You must have been dreaming some one heck of a dream," Jackson informed her.

"Why? Hope I didn't snore or something," Max responded.

"No. No snoring, but you sure did jerk around a lot. My Momma used to do the same thing when she had nightmares. Want to talk about it?" she asked.

"Not really," Max answered back.

"I understand," Jackson replied.

The rest of the trip to Royal Oaks was made in silence. Max stared out of the window at the passing trees as their branches were dropping colorful leaves onto the ground. She remembered how much fun she had with her daughter in the fall, and the silly costumes she made her for Halloween. She also remembered how long the winters last in Minnesota. Her reverie then turned fondly to how long the summers were in California, which reminded her to give her daughter a call when she got home. It had been awhile since she last talked to her.

Arriving back to Royal Oaks in time for shift change, she went through the shift change routine. She then settled in for what she hoped would be a quiet evening. Sitting back in her office, she decided to go to the hospital in the morning and check on Randall's condition, hoping there would be some good news.

There were several messages waiting for her, one being from Tom Edwards, the Hennepin County medical examiner, asking her to call him back when convenient. She didn't know if he had good or bad news. She resolved to call him in the morning after visiting the hospital.

She got her wish for a quiet night. Except for a drunk and disorderly and a few traffic stops, the night and early morning were uneventful. After morning shift change, she went home and slept in until after lunch. Grabbing a snack, she then headed to the hospital. Arriving there, she located Randall's doctor, to ask for an update. The doctor informed her that although John's wounds were healing nicely, the swelling in his skull was not responding to the drugs they were giving him, and until the swelling went down, they were going to keep him in the coma until they see positive results from the medication, even if it took a month or two more.

Dejected from the news the doctor had given her, she sat in her car and called Tom Edwards on his cell phone.

"Chief, I have some news. Can we meet?" he asked.

"Where and when?" Max responded.

"SVR campgrounds- tonight. Incognito," he told her, mysteriously.

"Sure," she answered back, and then remembering she had duty, she replied. "is this official business or other?"

"Very official. There's someone I want you to meet. She doesn't want anyone knowing she is talking to the police. So, therefore it's all hush-hush. Do you need anything to disguise yourself?" Tom questioned.

Max almost said no, but then remembered the wedding dress she had worn at Ms. Nelson's wedding. "Yes, I have something I can wear," she responded.

"Great. I'll meet you at the SVR campground, by the front stockade gate at ten thirty tonight. Okay?" Edwards said.

"Got it," Max shot back.

Going back to her apartment, she located the Viking dress still hanging in her closet. She put it in the trunk of her squad car. She then proceeded to lay down for an afternoon nap. Before she drifted off, she wondered if she should take one of her officers with her but decided against it as she would have Tom Edwards as her babysitter.

Saturday shift change went smooth and again she hoped for a quiet night. The evening seemed to last forever until finally it got close to nine o'clock. Informing dispatch that she was going out on patrol, she headed out the back door of the police building to her squad car. Taking the Viking dress out of the trunk, she proceeded to change into it in a storage shed next to the police building, so that no one could see her.

Driving out to the fair site, she took her PTSD medication just in case there were campfires burning on site. It was a good thing she did because as she drove on to the site, she could see the smoke of many campfires hanging low to the ground like a fog. Parking her car as close as she could to the employee entrance, she proceeded to walk through the gate and into the campgrounds of the SVR.

She was surprised at the number of people on the premises, all of them dressed in Viking garb. Many families were sitting around campfires either eating or drinking out of medieval looking plates, goblets, and mugs. Conversations and some singing created a constant sound in the background.

As she walked past the longhouse, she saw where the hole in the wall caused by the explosion had been repaired. Making her way to the front gate, she was good-naturedly propositioned by several of the men passing by, who were obviously very drunk. They offered her beer and bed, which she politely refused and kept walking. Approaching the gate, it became hard to see details in the night as there were no campfires to provide illumination. The one thing she could easily see was her breath condensing in the cold night air as she walked along. Reaching the gate, she observed several men standing in the dark, smoking cigarettes. Upon seeing her, one of the men put out his cigarette and approached her. It was Tom Edwards.

Upon recognizing him, she let out a sigh of relief.

"I'm glad it's you and not another Viking with a proposition," she said with a whisper.

"Did you get a lot of offers?" he whispered back.

"Too many," Max replied.

"Don't worry. Most of them are a harmless bunch. They're just letting off a little steam before they go back to their wives and kids. They would probably be shocked if you took them up on their offer," Tom whispered back with a smile.

"Are your wife and boys here?" Max asked softly.

"Yeah, they're back at our camp, but they're not who we are going to see. I got someone else who wants to talk to you," Tom whispered to her as he signaled her to follow him.

Walking back into the campground, Max carefully scanned the people standing around, hoping that there wasn't anybody there that could recognize her. Suddenly she felt a hand squeeze her buttocks. Startled, she swung around and slapped the face of the huge, burly man who had groped her. It only took a second before Tom Edwards was between her and her assailant.

"What the hell, Olaf?" Tom angrily spit out, getting into the other man's face.

Putting his offending hand on his mouth where a small trickle of blood was starting to flow, the offending man replied, "Sorry, Eric. I saw her alone here earlier and I thought she came back to take me up on my offer."

"You drunk?" Tom questioned.

"Yeah, kinda," the burly man slurred.

"You know the rules. Now get back to your camp and sober up," Tom ordered.

By this time there was a small crowd of onlookers starting to gather around the scene. Max noticed them and realized this was the one thing she didn't need, too much attention.

Putting her hand on Tom's arm, she said, "It's okay, we need to go. Now," nodding her head toward the gathering crowd. Tom looked around and realized that she was right. Taking her hand, he led her away from the gathering crowd.

Walking a distance away, he took her to one of the peasant huts that had been built for the campers. Tom knocked on the door and a woman responded from inside, "Eric?" the woman asked.

"Yes, it's me," Tom replied.

"Come in," the voice answered.

Opening the door, he led Max into a small room with a cot, a table, and a couple of chairs.

It was illuminated by several candles scattered throughout the room. A small fire was burning in the corner fireplace, throwing off welcoming heat from the chilly night. A small, petite woman was sitting on the edge of the cot. "Is this her?" the woman asked Tom.

"Yes, this is her," he responded. "Tell her what you know." The woman took a deep breath as Tom and Max sat in the two chairs by the table.

"First of all, my name is Sarah, Sarah Redmond. My boyfriend was Ron Sorenson, one of the victims in the explosion in the long house. I want to give you some information that might help in your investigation," she explained.

"Go on," Max replied.

"First, I want to say that Ron was a good man, but with the economy the way it is, being a car salesman wasn't making him too much money. Most of the time he was broke, but he got by. Then one day, a week before he died, he suddenly had money. A lot of money. I asked him where it came from but all he told me was that it was a down payment for doing a job for a guy. When I asked him about the job, he told me it was something special here at the Medieval fair," she explained.

"Did he say who the man was?" Max asked.

"No, but he did say he was an angel from heaven. A fat angel with a toupee," she replied.

"A fat angel with a toupee?" Max questioned.

"Yes, that was exactly how he described him," Sarah responded.

The first person who came into Max's mind was Jack Taylor, the owner of the Hummer in Bemidji. Rising from her chair, Max thanked Sarah for her help as she and Tom headed for the door.

Just as they reached the door, Sarah asked, "I saw on TV there was a reward offered for information on the case. Is there any chance that my information might qualify?"

Max turned to her and said, "It might, it just might. I'll let you know."

As they slowly headed back to the parking lot, Max asked, "I have a stupid question. Why does everyone call you Eric?"

"Everybody in the society has a persona name, Eric Silverhand is mine," he replied. Max nodded her head in acknowledgment but didn't really understand.

Chapter 28

Max proceeded to drive back to the police station. She then proceeded to change out of her Viking dress and back into her uniform in the storage shed, before going back into the station house. Notifying dispatch that she was back in the building, she sat in her office and pondered how she was going to be able to use the information she had been given, without the mayor firing her for violating her conflict-of-interest situation. In the end, Tom Edwards saved her from the problem.

When she turned on her computer there was an email from Tom, detailing everything that had been discovered at the Viking village that evening, except her name had been neatly removed. She noticed that he had also forwarded the message to Mayor Price, with the same content. She made a mental note to thank Tom later.

Max settled behind her desk for the rest of the shift, taking care of the paperwork from the last couple days. After the end of her shift, she headed back to her apartment for some breakfast and some sleep. When she woke up in the early afternoon, she noticed a message from the mayor's office, asking her to drop in and see him sometime in the afternoon at her convenience. Max was sure that he wanted to discuss the new information that Tom Edwards had provided.

About three o'clock, Max put on her uniform and headed to the mayor's office. Arriving, she was ushered into his office. Mayor Price was holding a sheet of paper in his hand.

"I assume that you got the same report that I did?" the mayor asked.

"I did. It looks like we got our first solid lead in the case," Max replied.

"Good, make sure that your Deputy Chief gets a copy so he can follow up on it. Okay?" the mayor requested.

"Sure will, Mayor," Max responded,

"Oh, and a couple of small matters, I'm going to need you to take care of." he replied.

"Sure thing, what do you need?" she questioned.

"For some reason the security camera in the police parking lot seems to have quit working last night. You'll need to get it fixed, and you'll also need to send an officer out to the Viking village and investigate a disturbance between a drunken Viking and a woman that took place last night," he instructed, with a very large grin.

Max immediately turned red, knowing that the mayor knew everything she did from the previous evening. *How does he know this stuff?* Max thought. "I'll take care of it immediately," was all she said as she hurriedly left his office.

Returning to the police building, she found Deputy Wilson at his desk working on paperwork. As she approached, he quickly slid several papers he was looking at into the top drawer of his desk.

"Good afternoon, Chief. You're here early," he addressed her, nervously.

"Good afternoon to you. Looks like you're staying busy," she replied.

"Yeah, always something to do. What's up?" he inquired.

"I was wondering if you got the bank statements on our two victims from the fair, yet?" she questioned.

"I sure did," he responded, looking for a piece of paper on his desk. Finding it, he read it to her.

"It looks like both had a cash infusion into their accounts at about the same time. Ron Sorenson had put almost ten thousand dollars into his checking account. Ron Newgate put five thousand in his checking and five thousand in his savings," he read off the paper.

"So, both received ten thousand dollars at about the same time?" Max asked.

"It appears so," he responded, checking the dates on the paper he was holding.

"Good job," Max stated, realizing that the bank statements verified Sorenson's girlfriend's statement from the previous night.

"Thanks, Chief," Wilson replied. Then pausing for a moment or two, he seemed mentally convoluted. Finally, opening his desk drawer, he proceeded to take the papers he had previously concealed when Max walked in, out of the drawer.

"Look Chief, I have to tell you something. I've been with the department for over five years and your Deputy Chief for almost a year, and I have never been happier," he explained to her.

"But?" Max asked, almost knowing what was coming.

"But, with the new baby arriving soon and the cost of everything going up, I need to make a change in my life as far as my employment. I've received a letter from the city of Blaine, offering me the Chief of Police position, and I'm really torn between staying here or taking the offer. I really respect you, and I would really appreciate your advice. What do you think I should do?" he pleaded.

"Well, I think you should do what's best for you and your family. But first let me talk to the mayor and see if we can find more money for you. If not, I would be more than willing to give you a great going away party. I think you'd make a great Chief of Police either here or in Blaine. Can you give me a week or two, before you make up your mind? I'll talk to the mayor tomorrow and get back to you as soon as possible. Okay?" Max stated.

"Thanks Chief. I really appreciate your help. I need to make my decision by the fifteenth of November, so we do have some time," Wilson told her.

"Good. Let me see what I can do," Max stated, then walked into her office to contact the mayor for an appointment for the following day. After making the appointment, she made a call to Mark Richards.

"What can I do for you, Chief?" Richards asked her.

"Need a favor," Max replied.

"Shoot," he replied back.

"Can you access someone's bank account, discreetly without them knowing it?" Max asked.

"Who's the someone?" Mark asked.

"It's a Mr. Jack Taylor from Bemidji Minnesota," she stated.

"What are you looking for?" he asked again.

"A twenty to thirty-thousand-dollar withdrawal in the last month or two," she replied.

"Consider it done. Talk to you later. Okay?" Mark stated.

"Okay, and thanks," Max concluded.

Chapter 29

The following day, Max went to her appointment with the mayor. She explained the situation to him about her deputy. He was sympathetic but explained that although the town budget could give him a raise, it wouldn't be anywhere close to the salary of a chief of police. He did explain to her that if her deputy left, she'd probably be able to hire another officer to the police force and promote one of her other officers to deputy chief.

Max considered the mayor's statement and resolved herself to the fact that she was probably going to lose her deputy chief. That meant more lost time training someone new for the job.

Heading back to the police building, she resolved to try and make the transition as smooth as possible.

Arriving at her office, she saw that Mark Wilson had called and asked her to call back as soon as possible. Closing the door to her office, she dialed him up on her cellphone.

"You're not going believe what I found," Wilson exclaimed, excitedly.

"You hit paydirt?" Max questioned.

"Oh yeah, and a whole lot more, I think," he replied.

"What you got?" Max responded curiously.

"Well to start with, Mr. Taylor is moving a lot of money in and out of his different accounts, and he has a lot of them. Over the last year he has made over one and three quarter of a million dollars from his business ventures. I checked the dates of his deposits alongside the dates of his flight from his Mexico airport, and each one of his sizable deposits match exactly with his return to Bemidji. He's not even trying to hide the money transfers," Mark explained.

"What does your gut tell you?" Max inquired.

"I'm guessing he's bringing something back from Mexico, that's worth a lot of money," Mark explained.

"Drugs?" Max asked.

"Yup," Mark replied, then continued on, "it's a perfect set up. He owns his own airfield in Mexico and then uses a small airport like Bemidji, where he knows he won't be questioned too much when he comes back into the United States. My only question is, why isn't his plane searched when he comes back here?"

Max thought for a moment, then responded, "Maybe it was, at first. Last year I was interviewing a prisoner at the Texas prison system in Huntsville. When I asked him about his smuggling operation, he told me a story. I think I remember it," She paused, recounting how the story went.

"There once was an American border crossing guard named Jim and a Mexican smuggler named Juan. Once a week, Juan would cross the border from Mexico into the United States with a backpack and riding a bicycle. Jim knew that Juan was smuggling so he searched Juan, his backpack and took the bike apart, looking for what Juan was carrying, but each time, Jim found nothing. This went on, once a week for years.

Juan would cross; Jim would search, always with the same conclusion-nothing.

Finally, one day Jim retired and shortly after, so did Juan. A couple of months later, Jim walks into a bar and sees Juan sitting there with a drink, all alone. He goes up to Juan and buys him a drink, and then Juan buys Jim a drink.

So, they're sitting in this bar for several hours, getting good and drunk. Eventually, Jim asked Juan, "Juan, every time you crossed the border at my station, I knew you were smuggling something, but I could never find anything. Please, as an amigo, tell me what it was you were smuggling. I promise, you won't get into trouble. I've just got to know," Juan finishes his drink, and as he looks Jim in the eye, he smiles. All he said was..."

"Bicycles," Mark finished her story.

"Aww, you heard it before?" Max exclaimed.

"Yeah, that story is older than dirt, and probably just an urban legend. But there is a grain of truth in it. After a while, inspectors get complacent doing the same inspection over and over again and start overlooking the obvious. Perhaps that's what happened to Mr. Taylor," Mark explained.

"Could be, but what about the money transfers? What did you find out about them?" Max asked.

"Plenty. Looking at the amount of cash transfers you were asking about, Taylor transferred thirty thousand from one of his accounts into his girlfriend's checking account and that very same day, just ten days before the robbery and explosion, she then wrote a check for cash, out of her account for that exact same amount. Is that what you're looking for?" he asked.

"Exactly," Max exclaimed. "It proves that there were three men involved in the theft. Two of the victims were killed and a third took the stone and drove the Hummer away. But in the end, it is all just really circumstantial. No hard evidence. There isn't any real proof that the money was used to hire the three men."

"True, but you might be able to squeeze Taylor if he were to get busted on drug possession. Right?" he suggested.

"That might work. Taylor seems like the type who wouldn't do well in prison. I might just have an idea of how to squeeze him to talk," Max replied, excited at the prospect.

"Great. If you need any help, just let me know. By the way, have you got any news on John? I haven't had much of a chance to get to the hospital for the last few days. How's he doing?" Mark asked.

"The last time I checked, he was still the same. The doctor said that they were considering bringing him out of the coma in a week or two if the swelling in his head continues to go down. They're trying some new type of wonder drug, and the doctor said it looked promising," Max explained.

"Great news. Keep me upgraded if anything changes. I won't have a chance to see him until after the election coming up, next week. Got to go. Talk later," Mark told her as he hung up the phone.

"Bye and thank you," she responded, as she hung up the phone.

Chapter 30

Max started formulating her plan to find out if Jack Taylor was responsible for the explosion and theft at the Medieval fair. The first part involved figuring out how to find out what type of illegal activity he was conducting, and the second part was using that information to get a confession out of him about the theft.

The one main question that troubled her was why he would commit such a crime. She hoped that the answers would come with his confession. The next problem was how to inform the mayor what she had discovered, and how she found it. She figured he wouldn't be happy about her methods and involvement.

One other problem she had was she knew she was also going to have to confide in her deputy chief and give him the news about not getting a raise. Deputy Chief Edwards took the news better than she expected. He said he was pretty sure what the mayor's response was going to be and had already made up his mind to take the job in Blaine. Max asked him if he had any recommendations for his replacement. Mark suggested Curtis Jenkins as his replacement. Max knew Curtis and agreed with his choice.

"When do you start in Blaine?" Max queried.

"I'll notify them today that I'll take their job. I'm sure you'll want me to help train him and get him up and running. You know Officer Jenkins is familiar with the job as he was my right-hand man when you were in Texas last year. So how does right after the election is over for the changeover sound to you?" Mark asked her.

"Sounds good to me," Max responded. "I'm really going to miss you," she said pensively.

"Yeah, me too. But on the bright side, we'll only be thirty minutes from each other," Mark added.

That information put Max more at ease. She made herself a mental note to contact Human Resources, to start the application process for a new replacement deputy. Her next phone call was to Chief Cooke in Bemidji. As the phone call to Chief Cooke was ringing, Max contemplated how she was going to broach the subject delicately. Finally, Chief Cooke answered the phone.

"Hello, Chief Cooke. It's Chief Somers from the Royal Oaks Police Department," she started the conversation

"Nice to hear from you again, Chief Somers. What can I help you with, today?" Chief Cooke asked.

"I need a big favor," Max stated.

"Name it," Chief Cooke replied.

"Look, I don't know how to ask it, so I'll just get to the point. I would like you to take a good look at Jack Taylor's plane. I've got a feeling that he's shipping more than clients and cargo from Mexico," Max explained to her.

"Hold your breath, Chief. I've already checked him out. In fact, TSA and DEA has had their eyes on him for several months. As far as we can tell, he's clean. All he's bringing into the country are passengers and legitimate cargo," Chief Cooke told her.

Disappointed, Max asked, "You're sure?"

"Sorry, but yes. We've checked him multiple times over the last three months, and each time we've found nothing out of the ordinary. He flies his Lear jet from Bemidji to south Mexico and coming back, stops for fuel in Waco, Texas and then back to Bemidji. We thought maybe something might be dropped off at the Waco stop but airport surveillance videos show he doesn't even get out of the plane. He just refuels and takes back off. I can send you the videos if you like." Chief Cooke explained to her.

Max felt all the air go out of her as Chief Cooke explained the situation to her. Dejectedly, she replied.

"Thanks Chief. I would appreciate any help you can provide."

"No problem. Any time. I just sent the videos to your phone. By the way, his flight manifest shows he's expected back from Mexico tomorrow. If you'd like, you can participate in the inspection of his plane," she stated.

"No, but I really appreciate your help," Max told her, as she hung up the phone.

Her phone beeped to inform her that the videos had arrived. She downloaded the videos onto her computer. She then proceeded to view the videos Chief Cooke provided to her. Some of the videos were of the of the security people, inspecting Taylor's Lear jet upon arrival in Bemidji. Others are of the plane being refueled in Waco. The refueling process appeared to be normal as the plane would taxi up to a fuel truck and then immediately take off with no one exiting the plane. Max viewed the videos several time looking for any clue that might answer what was going on.

Suddenly, she realized something. The same thing happened each time the plane was refueled. Calling Mark Richards at Randall Security, she asked him, "Mark, how far is San Antonio from Waco?"

"About an hour drive. Why?" He asked.

"I remember you saying that your new offices were in San Antonio. Right? she asked.

"Right, and again, why? Mark questioned.

"Look, I've been watching videos of our suspected smuggler, Jack Taylor, refuel his Lear jet at the Waco airport. Each time he arrives at the tarmac, the fuel truck pulls up to the plane and blocks the view of the plane from the security camera. And the other thing is, I researched the range of the Lear jet. It can easily travel from Bemidji to Playa Del Carmen without having to refuel. So why would it have to refuel coming back from Mexico?" Max questioned.

"Good catch," Mark responded. "I can get one of my associates from our office in San Antonio to get over there and do a closer inspection the next time he flies in."

"That would be tomorrow," Max informed him.

"Excellent. If anything is going on, my people will figure it out," Mark said confidently.

"How? If he spots anything out of the ordinary, he will probably rabbit and head down a hole," Max inquired.

"He'll never see a thing. I promise you," Mark stated.

"How?" Max asked.

"You've never heard of a drone? We have one that can photograph a pimple on a bug's butt from a half a mile in the sky. He'll never know it's there. If anything is going on, we'll catch it," Mark stated.

Chapter 31

After a restless night, Max awoke the next morning. She decided to go to the hospital and check on Randall's progress. After the visit and finding no change in his condition, she decided to try and get a hold of Assumpta. After several attempts, she finally got through to her. Assumpta was pleased to hear from Max but explained to her that she was on the road, doing campaigning for the upcoming election.

"How are you doing in the polls?" Max asked.

"Russell is coming on strong, but I think it's too little, too late. It would take a miracle for him to pull it off. So just to be on the safe side, Lars has arranged a bunch of campaign stops over the next seven days." Assumpta stated.

"Well, if you do any stops anywhere close to Royal Oaks, maybe we could do lunch and talk about that job offer, we discussed earlier?" Max inquired.

"Made up your mind?" Assumpta questioned.

"Maybe." Max replied. "I need answers to a couple of questions first."

"Okay then, I'll make a point of being in your neighborhood in a couple of days," she replied back.

"Sounds good. Give me a call before you come, so I can clear my schedule, Okay?" Max stated.

"Will do. Don't forget to vote," Assumpta added.

"After her conversation with Assumpta, Max waited on pins and needles the rest of the morning and well into the middle of the afternoon. She spent her time cleaning her apartment. About two thirty, the phone call she had been anticipating came on her cell phone. It was a text message from Mark Richards.

'Got it. See you in forty minutes,' was all it said. Max was kind of upset that he didn't give any more information but figured he must have had good reasons not to reveal any of it on the phone. Waiting patiently, she felt a sense of anticipation when she heard a knock at her apartment door.

Letting Mark in, she noticed a broad grin on his face. "Good news?" she asked, excitedly.

"Good news," he replied. Setting his laptop computer on her kitchen table, he proceeded to pull up the videos recorded earlier in the day in Waco. Max and Mark huddled around the laptop so they could both see the video screen.

"This first video was taken from the airport's CCTV, aimed at the arriving runway," he explained.

He and Max stared intently as the video showed a Lear jet landing and taxiing up to the tarmac. Finally stopping, a tanker truck full of jet fuel pulled up beside the plane, effectively visually blocking a good portion of the plane. They watched as two men got out of the truck and proceeded to fill the plane with fuel. Because of the position of the tanker, nothing could be seen of them as they disappeared behind the truck.

"This is a carbon copy of the videos I've already seen," Max told Mark.

"Bet you didn't see this video," he told Max as he pulled up the next video. She observed a video of a camera mounted on a helicopter type drone rising into the air. She recognized the aerial view as it approached the scene of the tanker truck approaching the stopped plane. The recording displayed the two men getting out of the tanker. She watched as one of the men proceeded to hook a hose from the tanker onto the fuel intake on the plane.

As this was going on, the other man went to the fuselage of the plane and proceeded to stealthily open the side cargo door. He then quickly removed two suitcase- size parcels and transferred them into a side compartment of the truck.

Amazed at the detail of the recording, Max asked Mark, "They never saw the drone?"

"Nope. That drone was almost three thousand feet high. I even had to get FAA approval to use it at the airport." Mark explained. "That video looks like it was taken from twenty feet away, doesn't it?" Mark bragged.

"It sure does, and did I just see a drug drop?" she asked.

"Don't know yet, but we will when the DEA apprehends them trying to move those parcels off the airport property. They and the packages are now under twenty-four-hour surveillance," Mark explained.

"We got him," Max exclaimed, as she sat back on her kitchen chair.

"Not yet, but as soon as I get confirmation on the cargo, then you can go get him," Mark told her.

"One thing puzzles me. We didn't see any exchange between anybody on the plane and the two men. How does the money exchange hands?" she asked him.

"Electronic transfer. There were a bunch of transfers from a bank in Cancun into Taylor's accounts. I noticed them when I accessed his multiple accounts in Bemidji," Mark explained.

"Makes sense," Max stated then added, "Mark, this was some really excellent detective work. I must ask if I can I have copy of the video? I'm going to have to show it to my boss when we have confirmation of arrest.

"Mayor Price is still wanting me to have a babysitter, as far as the Medieval fair investigation, and I don't know how I'm going to explain this to him," Max said.

"Do you want me to talk to him? I know that you know that John has some high-level contacts in Washington. What you don't know is that I share the same contacts, what with John incapacitated. I guess I would qualify as your babysitter," Mark offered.

Max felt a wave of relief as Mark made the offer. "Fantastic, but it won't ruin your confidentiality, will it?" 'she asked.

"I think it will be okay. I'll see if I can work around your conflict-of-interest problem, too," Mark replied.

"Sounds good. Sounds very good," Max responded.

"Okay, I'll contact you as soon as the results are in from Waco, and then you can take care of business here. I'll also make a call to Washington and hopefully have some people square things with your mayor." Mark reassured.

"Thanks Mark, I really appreciate all the help," Max said gratefully.

Chapter 32

The call from Mark came in the next morning. The two drivers of the fuel tanker at the Waco airport had not wasted any time in trying to remove the packages from the airport. Mark explained that they were apprehended in the airport parking lot, trying to put the two packages into the trunk of one of their cars.

Mark told her they both claimed they had found the packages in the airport and as good citizens, were taking them to the police station. Testing proved that the packages contained high grade heroin.

When shown the video that Mark's associate had taken with the drone, they both knew they had been busted and changed their story very quickly.

Hoping to cut a deal, they both rolled over on Jack Taylor, confessing to having cooperated with the drug smuggling plot for about six months, and offered to testify against him.

"You got him!" Mark exclaimed on the phone. "Now it's time to squeeze him."

"Yes, it is. Yes, it is," Max replied, almost starting to cry.

Now to turn the screws on Mr. Jack Taylor, Max thought to herself.

Getting off the phone with Mark, she next made a phone call to Chief Cooke in Bemidji.

"Chief Cooke, I need to you arrest Mr. Jack Taylor on drug smuggling charges," Max told her.

"You got proof?" Chief Cooke asked.

"Video and confessions from two of his accomplices. I'll send you a copy of the arrest warrant that I'll be issuing today, along with copies of the video and the confessions that were obtained," Max informed her.

"Sounds great, but this really is your bust. Are you sure you don't want to execute the arrest? Cooke asked.

"Thanks, Chief but I'm buried with work here. However, I am sending two of my officers up to you to escort him back to Royal Oaks. We need to ask him some questions about a homicide case here that he might have information on. After we are done with him, you can have him back for prosecution," Max explained to her.

"It's a deal," Cooke replied. "Send me the warrant and the other evidence, and I'll release him to your deputies when they get here."

"Thanks, Chief," Max told her.

"No, thank you, Chief Somers, and by the way-congratulations," Chief Cooked told her.

Hanging up the phone, Max proceeded to have Deputy Edwards assign two deputies to travel up to Bemidji to bring Jack Taylor back to Royal Oaks. Mark decided to send officers Curtis Jenkins and the rookie, Hall. She then had the arrest warrant issued and sent to Bemidji along with copies of the confessions and videos.

Jenkins and Hall got back from Bemidji around eight o'clock that evening. Even though Max was on the day shift, she waited for them to arrive at the station with Jack Taylor. Upon their arrival at the police station, Taylor started immediately demanding a lawyer. Max told him he could make his phone call in the morning. Taylor was not happy about having to spend the night in the Royal Oaks holding cell.

Max took great pleasure in turning the key to the jail cell door and letting him stew in his protestation, overnight.

The next morning, after the shift change, she took Taylor to an interrogation room and let him make his phone call. Around noon a lawyer from Minneapolis showed up, wishing to see his new client. After about an hour of consulting with Taylor, the lawyer terminated the interview and asked to see Max.

"What are you charging my client with?" he asked her.

"Illegal transportation of controlled substances, narcotic possession, money laundering, bribery, and when we've completed our investigation, assault, deadly assault, illegal possession of explosives, and theft," Max said, rolling off the litany of charges,

The lawyer smiled, and asked, "Maybe you left out beating his dog?"

"Very funny," Max replied to him, "But we got a pretty solid case with our evidence."

"Which I would like to see as soon as possible." He demanded, continuing, "When is the arraignment?"

"He will see the local magistrate tomorrow morning and the Feds want him the following day. So, my guess is up and till then, he'll be staying with us. A copy of everything we have will be sent to your office later today. Will that work?" Max explained to him, not telling him that his client would be going to Bemidji for eventual prosecution.

"Yes, that should just about do it," the lawyer replied, then added, "Until then, I have advised my client to remain silent. Understood?"

"Perfectly," Max responded.

Chapter 33

The next morning, Max went to visit Randall at the hospital, hoping for a change in his condition. There wasn't any different news from his doctor. He explained to her that the new medication seemed to be reducing the swelling, but it was slow going. However, he did tell her that with the progress of getting the swelling of the brain down, they might consider taking him out of the coma in a week or two.

The doctor explained to her that even ending the coma, there might be residual brain damage and physical therapy to contend with once he was conscious again. This news put her into a bad mood.

Going to the police station, Max was determined to get a confession out of Taylor any way she could. Before having him transferred to the interrogation room, she made sure that there was a television and VCR player hooked up to it, along with a digital camera mounted on a tripod in order to record the interview.

Max took Mark Wilson with her into the room to act as the operator of the video recorder and also as a witness to the interrogation.

Upon entering the room and sitting across the table from Taylor, she explained to him what was happening.

"You understand the charges against you, Mr. Taylor?" she asked.

"Yes," was all he said.

"You understand that this conversation is being recorded and that you have the right to remain silent, that anything you say can be used against you in court. You have the right to an attorney, and if you can't afford an attorney, one will be appointed for you," Max explained.

"Yes," He repeated.

"The first thing I am going to show you Mr. Taylor, is a video of your plane landing at the Waco, Texas airport. Mr. Taylor, can you identify the Lear jet landing at the Waco airport?" she asked him as she nodded to Mark to push the play button on the VCR sitting on the table. The video on the television showed his Lear jet approaching and landing on the runway, and the tanker truck pulling up to the plane. Stopping the video, she asked again, "Sir, is that your plane?"

"It appears to be," he replied, reluctantly.

Turning back on the video, she asked. "And can you see what these two men are doing?"

Staring at the video, Taylor proceeded to turn red in the face, and started to sweat. "No comment," was his reply.

Max pulled a couple of booking photographs of two men in the video from her folder and showed then to Taylor.

"And do you recognize these two men?" she asked, smiling at his discomfort.

Again, his response was, "No comment," as he started squirming in his chair.

Then taking a couple of pages of typed notes out of the folder, she asked, "Would you like to see the analysis report from the content of the two suitcases taken from your plane and the confessions of the two individuals shown in the photographs?"

"Damn, it's hot in here. Is the air conditioning on?" Taylor asked, starting to sweat profusely.

Max and Mark looked at each other and smiled. "Sir, it's the first of November. We don't run air conditioning this time of year," Mark commented.

"Perhaps our guest would like some water?" Max suggested. Mark shut off the recorder, rose from his chair and left the room to obtain some bottled water for Taylor. As soon as Mark was out of the interrogation room, Max started the real interrogation.

"Well Mr. Taylor, I think you would have to admit that the evidence is pretty conclusive. Just for your information, I've notified the DEA of your activity and sent them the evidence we have. When they get through with you, you'll be spending fifteen to twenty years in a federal lock-up, but maybe out in five to ten, with good behavior.

Look. I really don't care much about your drug problem, but what I do care about is your involvement with the death of two people, the injury of a third and the theft of the Kensington stone.

I know you were involved, as we have your paper trail hiring the men involved, and your Hummer used in the theft. Now, in this state, that means Stillwater prison for the rest of your life once you get out of the federal prison."

Taylor appeared to get more distraught as Max him told him the scenario of what was going to happen to him.

He began to break down and started sobbing, putting his head in his hands. Just then Mark came into the room with a bottle of water. Looking at Taylor crying and then at Max, he asked, "Is he alright?"

Max just smiled and told him, "Yeah, I just gave him a reality check."

"Mark, turn on the recorder. I think Mr. Taylor is going to give us a statement now," Max requested.

Mark went to his chair and proceeded to turn the camera back on. Taylor raised his head from the table and dried his eyes with the sleeve of his shirt. Taking the bottle of offered water, he proceeded to drink half of the bottle down.

"What can you do for me?" he questioned.

"With the Feds, nothing, but with our case, I'm sure it can get pled down to assault and burglary. With luck and maybe some testimony at your sentencing about your cooperation, you might only get five to ten years. With a sympathetic judge you might get your sentence to run concurrent," Max explained.

"Wait, what does that mean-concurrent?" Taylor asked.

"It means that your sentence could be served at the same time as your federal sentence," Mark expounded.

Mr. Taylor sat silent for a second, then he suddenly drank the last of the water from the bottle, then asked,

"What do you want to know?"

Max and Mark looked at each other, then Max started, "It was your Hummer used in the Medieval fair robbery. Right?"

"Yes," was his response.

"You gave the vehicle to either Newgate, Sorenson, or a third person to use in the robbery. Correct?" Max stated.

"Yes," was Taylor's response again, "but I never told them to get drunk. Those idiots blew themselves up and dented my Hummer."

"Who was the third person involved?" Mark asked.

"I don't know. Newgate was going to hire another person to act as the driver. I never asked his name," Taylor explained.

"Where were they going to take the stone?" Max demanded.

"I don't know. Look, I was paid fifty thousand dollars to organize the job. All I had to do was hire the manpower and give them a sealed letter along with the money. That's what I did. When I gave the envelope and money to Newgate, he opened it up. I assumed it was the money and the instructions for the job. When he opened the envelope, he read it, looked closely at the envelope, and told me the note said that if the seal of the envelope was broken, they were to kill me," he told them shakily.

"That was all it took to scare the hell out of me. Newgate asked me where the keys for the Hummer were, and I told him where I put them in my office. After they left, I was done with them, and then I left for Mexico. That's all I know. When I got back from Mexico, the keys were back, and the Hummer was dented and scratched. My girlfriend noticed the damage on the Hummer immediately and reported it to the police before I could stop her. I think you know the rest," he concluded.

Mark then asked, "How did you get the envelope?"

It was mailed to me inside a manilla envelope along with my instructions," Taylor explained.

"Did you notice the return address?" Max asked.

"There wasn't one, bur the postmark was from a Minneapolis zip code," he replied.

"Do you remember the zip code?" Max requested.

"Yeah, 55402, Hennepin County. Look, that's all I really know. Are we done? My God, it's hot in here," he spoke as he proceeded to unbutton his shirt.

"I think that's about it for now," she concluded, signaling Mark to turn off the digital camera. She then went to the door of the interrogation room and called for one of the deputies to escort Taylor back to his cell.

After Taylor was out of the room, Mark went over to the thermostat mounted on the wall.

"What did you have it set at?" she asked.

"Ninety degrees," Mark replied. "Man, I was having a tough time not sweating. How did you manage to appear so cool?"

"Years of living in Los Angeles," she replied with a smile.

Chapter 34

The next day, two federal officers arrived and took Jack Taylor away. Max called his lawyer that afternoon, to inform him that his client was being transferred to federal jurisdiction in Bemidji. Since she was working the evening shift, she stayed after shift change to make her phone calls and to talk to Mark Edwards, her Deputy Chief.

"Well, we made good headway with our investigation of Jack Taylor, but we aren't any closer to finding the stone or our third person involved.

"I was discussing the case with my overly pregnant wife last night and was telling her some of the problems we were having, and she came up with a possible solution. She said that since the two victims were involved in the SVR, it would make sense that the third suspect might be too." Mark explained.

Max jumped on Mark's statement. "Of course! That makes perfect sense. Mark- give that wife of yours a big hug, but not too hard a hug. You don't want to induce labor on her."

"It might not hurt to try. She is really miserable these days," Mark stated.

"Isn't she due about now?" Max asked.

"She's a week overdue, and I have already told Curtis to be on alert, as he will have to fill in for me when she delivers," Mark expounded.

"Great, do you think Curtis is ready?" she asked.

"More than ready. Just like my wife," he said with a smile.

"Great. I guess I need to talk to our favorite neighborhood medical examiner, since he has the best inside knowledge of the SVR," she told him.

"Do you need any help, or one of the mayor's babysitters?" Mark asked.

"No, not for this," Max informed him.

"Okay, but make sure you get some sleep, or you're really going to be dragging by tomorrow morning," he told her.

"Thanks, will do," Max assured him.

After she was alone in her office, she placed a call to the Hennepin County Medical Examiner, Tom Edwards.

Getting him on the phone took several tries. On the fourth try, she heard him pick up the phone.

"Hello, Chief Somers. What can I do for you? Tom asked.

"Busy?" Max asked.

"I was up to my armpits in an intestine, up until a few minutes ago, but I'm free now. What can I do for you?" he responded.

"I need you to put your thinking hat on," Max said.

"Okay, what do you need?" he asked.

"Do you know of anybody in the SVR that seemed to come into a lot of money recently?" she inquired.

"Off the top of my head, no. Why?" Tom replied.

"Well, the evidence seems to point to three participants in the Kensington stone theft, and since two of the participants were SVR's, then we figured..."

"The third one must be also," Tom finished her sentence for her.

"Correct," Max exclaimed.

"Good hypothesis, and since there is only a week left of the fair season, I guess I better get out there and do some snooping around. You don't want to get dressed up and help me, do you?" Tom replied kiddingly.

"Hell no!" Max responded, "I barely got out of there the last time with my virginity intact. I'm not going to take a second chance."

Tom had a good chuckle over her response. "I guess you're right, but seriously, any idea who we might be looking for?"

Max thought for a moment, then replied. "I think that we're looking for somebody who can carry a two-hundred-pound rock by himself and knows how to drive. Also, the person might be flashing a lot of money around. I guess that eliminates about half of your membership."

"Sadly true," Tom replied, "so, I guess I'm going to the fairgrounds tonight, and to do your dirty work."

"Thanks Tom. I guess I owe you another one," Max told him, gratefully.

"Sure do, and one of these days I'm going to collect," he responded.

"I'm sure you will," was all Max said, as she ended the phone conversation.

The next morning Max got a call from Assumpta, telling her that she and Lars would be making a campaign stop in

Royal Oaks at around noon and if Max could have lunch with them after the campaign speech and media interviews were over. Max couldn't think of a reason why not.

Around noon Lars called and asked her to meet them at the auditorium of the local high school. Max waited there about a half an hour as Assumpta was greeted by a medium size crowd and members of the local media before going into the auditorium for what Max could only compare to a high school pep rally.

Afterwards, Assumpta asked Max to join her and Lars for lunch at a restaurant in the new shopping mall. Once seated and having placed their orders, it took Assumpta several minutes to unwind from all the happenings of the campaigning.

"You alright?" Max asked.

"Yeah," Assumpta replied. "It's just that it takes just about everything out of me these days to get through all this campaigning. I thought it was fun at first, but answering the same questions multiple times, every day is getting to me. Do you know how hard it is to keep smiling all day? This campaigning sucks." Continuing, "But enough about me. What can I do for you?" she asked.

"Well, I just wanted to let you know that if you're elected, I'll take your job offer," Max told her.

A smile came over Assumpta's face. "Not if, but when I'm elected, and fantastic. I'll make sure you don't regret it."

Just then Lars interrupted their conversation and told them to look at the big screen TV mounted in the restaurant.

On the screen was a photo of Ted Russell and the caption. 'State Attorney General, Ted Russell, to make major announcement the day before the election on Friday.'

"Do you think he's going to withdraw? He's got to know he's going to lose," Lars said laughingly.

"I doubt it. He's probably got some rabbit he's going to pull out of a hat to try and swing some votes," Assumpta stated.

"Are you worried?" Max questioned.

"I'm always worried. Russell is famous for his last-minute theatrics to try and sway an election. I only worry about what his ploy is this time," Assumpta replied.

"Guess we'll find out on Thursday," Lars retorted, finishing his lunch.

When Max got back to the police station, there was a message for her to call Tom Edwards. Calling him on her cell phone, the call went straight to his voice mail. Leaving a message meant all she could do was wait for him to respond.

She decided that while she was waiting, she would start writing her letter of resignation to the mayor for if or when she would be hired to lead the State Police. After several attempts at writing the letter, she finally gave up.

Just as she wadded up her last attempt and threw it in the waste basket, Tom called her back. She grabbed her cell and answered, "Tom? What have you got?" she demanded.

"A hell of a hangover. I spent most of last night at the mead hall, trying to get information for you," Tom replied.

"What's a mead hall?" Max asked.

"Think medieval bar," he said with a groan.

"I didn't know you drank," Max stated,

"I don't. At least not a lot. But I did get some information for you. Do you want to meet up or can we discuss it over the phone?" he queried.

"Phone," Max replied.

"Okay, here goes. Rumor has it that one of our fighters just purchased a complete set of new armor and helmet. Now that by itself doesn't raise any alarms, but my sources tell me that he also put a sizable down payment on a parcel of land over by Buffalo," Tom explained.

"Why is that significant?" Max asked, puzzled.

"Well, this person is a security guard at a warehouse facility in downtown Minneapolis. Unless he got one hell of a raise, or a sizable inheritance from a dead relative, he shouldn't be able afford those expenditures. My source says that he was even buying rounds for the house, in the mead hall, two nights ago," Tom informed her.

"Do you have a name for this sudden millionaire?" Max asked.

"Ragnar Gunnarsson, otherwise, mundanely known a Steve Nash." Tom informed her.

"Who is this informant of yours?' Max asked again.

"Remember Olaf?" Tom replied, after a pause.

"Olaf whose handprint is tattooed on my butt-Olaf?" Max retorted.

"One and the same," he explained. "Get enough mead in him and he'll tell you everything you want to know, and a lot of stuff you don't want to. I think you can check it all out yourself."

"Thanks Tom. I really appreciate your help with this." Max told him. "Go home, get some rest and I'll talk with you later."

"I don't know if I have a bed to go to. Wife is going to kill me since I haven't been home all night," Tom said with slight groan.

"You haven't been home yet?" Max asked in astonishment.

"Nope- no shape to drive. My God, that man can drink. Oh, and by the way, Olaf says he's in love with you," he told her.

Max began to blush a little.

Chapter 35

After getting off the phone with Tom, Max immediately got on the phone with Mark Richards. She gave him the information that Tom Edwards had given her. Mark quickly pulled up a background check and bank information on Mr. Nash on his computer.

"Well, he didn't put the money in the bank, but he sure is making some large purchases without bank funds to cover them. The only other option is, he is paying cash for them. Looking at his salary, there is no way he could fund those purchases without a loan or someone giving him the money," Mark stated. "Nope. No record of a loan on his financial data."

"So, he could be our third person?" Max questioned.

"I think he needs to be asked about his finances, that's for sure. And the other thing- what better place to hide a two-hundred-pound rock, than in a warehouse," he observed.

Max had to agree, and mentally began formulating a plan to talk to Mr. Nash.

She went over to the county court and obtained a search warrant for the warehouse that Steve Nash worked at just in case he didn't answer questions to her satisfaction. She then went to the mayor's office and updated him. He advised her to take lots of back up with her when she went to interrogate him, just in case.

"I certainly will," Max reassured him. She knew anyone who could carry a two-hundred-pound rock could be a handful if he didn't want to cooperate.

The next day, Max made a call to the Hennepin County Sheriff's office, requesting back up at the warehouse where Mr. Nash worked. She was told that the sheriff's department would provide four or five officers to assist her.

Driving into Minneapolis with two of her deputies, Max thought to herself that this hopefully might provide the answers to a senseless crime.

Arriving at the office of the warehouse where Nash worked, she had one of the employees working there page Nash to the office. While waiting for him to arrive, she proceeded to place the sheriff deputies down the hall and around the corner, so they couldn't be seen.

As soon as Nash walked through the office door and saw Max and her two deputies waiting there for him, he bolted back out the door, where he was met by the waiting sheriff deputies. Putting up a brief struggle, he was quickly subdued and handcuffed. From the size and build of Nash, Max was easily convinced that he would have no problem carrying a two-hundred-pound stone. Max immediately knew that they had the third person in the conspiracy.

"Why'd you run, Mr. Nash?" Max inquired.

"Parking tickets," was all he said.

"Cute," Max responded. "We're going to take you to Royal Oaks, where we're going to talk to you about a lot more than your parking tickets. Now we can do this the easy way or the hard way. Your choice, Mr. Nash. You choose."

It seemed like all the air suddenly went out of him as he realized that there was no way out of the situation. He knew he was busted.

"What do you want?" he dejectedly asked.

"I have a search warrant to search this facility for the Kensington stone. You can make it a lot easier on yourself if you tell us where it is," Max explained to him, taking the search warrant out of her pocket and showing it to him.

Fortunately, for all concerned, he agreed to lead them to the stone. Entering one of the storage units, the officers discovered an object wrapped in a blanket, lying on the concrete floor. There was nothing else in the unit.

Max proceeded to unwrap the object with the help of one of her deputies. It was the Kensington stone, and it appeared at first glance, to be undamaged.

"Take him away," she told the deputies. Thanking the assisting Hennepin County deputies for their assistance in the arrest and also for helping to load the stone into the back of her police SUV, they proceeded to head back to Royal Oaks. The trip back was completely in silence. Once back at the Royal Oaks Police Department, she had the charges read to him, he was given his Miranda rights, then booked and placed in a cell. She knew the only charge that they had for sure was possession of stolen property. She was pretty certain she was going to be adding more charges as the day went by.

The next morning, after shift change, she has a deputy escort Nash to the interrogation room. Since her deputy chief, Mark Wilson, was at the hospital with his very pregnant wife, waiting for her to deliver, she had deputy Hall sit in the room with her. She wasn't sure how the interrogation was going to go, so she decided to just wing it.

Before the interrogation, she placed several sheets of blank paper in a file folder and she put it on the table in the interrogation room.

After Nash got seated, Max had Hall turn on the video recorder, and then ask, while tapping on the fake folder with her finger. "Well Mr. Nash, tell me how you got possession of the Kensington stone."

"I think you know where it came from," he replied in a surly tone.

"Yeah, we do, but I want you to say it for the record," Max told him, again tapping on the folder.

"Okay, okay. I helped steal it from the Renaissance fair. There-satisfied?" he replied.

"You mean the Medieval fair, don't you?" Max questioned.

"Okay, Yeah, the Medieval fair. Happy?" Again, with a surely attitude.

"You really want to do it the hard way? Fine! I'll just tell you what we know. You and two of your friends were hired by a Mr. Jack Taylor and then took his Hummer from Bemidji Minnesota, drove it to the Medieval fair, broke into the fair, and blew a hole in the Viking exhibit and the took the stone.

"In the process, Mr. Sorenson and Mr. Newgate were killed and a Mr. John Randall severely injured. You then transported the stone to your warehouse where you work and returned the Hummer back to Bemidji. Does that about cover it?" Max explained, still tapping on the fake file folder.

"Pretty much it in a nutshell," Nash confirmed. He then asked, "What was the guy's name that got injured?"

"Randall, John Randall. You didn't know him?" Max asked.

"Nope. We were just about to blow the hole in the wall and the plastic case. when he just showed up. His yelling scared Newgate and Sorenson so badly that they forgot to protect themselves from the explosion. I was watching in the Hummer, so after the big blow, I ran from the vehicle and saw the three of them on the ground. Nobody was moving, so I just assumed they were dead. I grabbed the stone, carried it through the side hole the explosion made, loaded it into the Hummer and then took off. The rest you have figured out," he concluded, all the time watching Max tap the folder.

Max sat back in her chair and contemplated what she had just been told. Then she thought of another question and asked, "Why did Jack Taylor want the stone?"

"I don't think he did. I had the impression that someone else was pulling his strings," Nash told her. "He has a gambling problem and maybe a drug problem. I got the impression that he was into somebody for a lot of money," Nash explained.

Max was curious about the fair's security cameras being shut off and asked Nash about it. His response disappointed Max. "Taylor told me they would be shut off when we gave the signal. How he did it? I have no idea. You'll have to ask him," he concluded.

Max sat back again in her chair, "I guess we're done here. Deputy Hall, would you take Mr. Nash back to his cell?'

After the two of them had left the room, she thought, *Two steps forward and one step backwards. Looks like I need to talk with Mr. Taylor again.*

Chapter 36

The next morning, at shift change, Max noticed that her deputy chief was absent. When she asked his substitute, Curtis, who was known as a master of understatement, about his absence, all he said was, "Baby."

Before going to hospital to see Mark's wife and baby, and Randall, she decided to call the mayor and also Mark Richards to update them as far as what new developments had been discovered. The mayor was very congratulatory in his praise for Max making such inroads in solving the case and reassured her that she had the full backing of him and the city council. Mark Richards took her call almost immediately, anxious for any good news she might have.

Explaining to him how the apprehension and interrogation of Nash concluded, he told her that he could take another look at Jack Taylor's financial statements, and maybe discover where his money was coming from and going. Max hoped that maybe he could find out who, as Nash stated, was pulling the strings.

After getting off the phone, she stopped at a local florist and procured flowers for Mark Wilson's wife and new baby. She then headed to the Royal Oaks Hospital. Arriving at the hospital, she first went to the maternity ward and found Mark with his wife and new baby.

Congratulating him and his wife, she gave her the flowers, then told Mark to take as much time off that he needed. He reassured Max that he would be back in a couple of days, as his wife's mother was coming to stay with them and help out with the new baby. Max got the impression that he wasn't too thrilled about her visit.

After visiting the new family, she headed to the third floor to check on Randall's condition. Arriving at his room, she found his doctor finishing up his examine of Randall.

"Everything is looking great," he told her. "The new medication is working, the swelling is going down, and we are planning to bring him out of the coma in a couple of days as long as his progress continues."

For the first time in a long time, Max started to feel optimistic about his recovery. After the doctor's news, Max headed back to her apartment, she made some lunch and took a nap. Once again, she dreamt about Randall and her in bed, and once again the dream ended as a horror story. Sitting straight up in bed from the dream and sweating profusely, she was visibly shaken and thought she was losing her mind. *How can I be having this dream? He's getting better. He's coming home to me. He's safe-I'm safe, so why this feeling of dread coming over me?* She thought to herself.

Getting out of bed, her first thought was to call Assumpta, but realizing that the election was the next day, she knew it would be impossible to contact her. Instead, she called the hospital and asked for Randall's nurse. Inquiring into Randall's wellbeing, she was told that there was no change since she had seen him earlier in the day.

Hanging up the phone, she felt a sense of relief. "Just nerves." She spoke out loud, "Just a bad case of nerves and being overly tired."

After taking a shower, and getting dressed, she was preparing to go back to the station house and finish up the paperwork on the Kensington stone, when her cell phone rang. Answering it, she was surprised to find Assumpta on the other end.

"I thought you were campaigning full time today?" Max questioned.

"Turn on your TV," she told Max.

Max reached for her television remote and turned it on. On the screen was Ted Russell conducting a news interview.

"...and my opponent has picked as her head of the State Police, a policewoman who was investigated for the cold-blooded murder of her fellow police officer. This woman just also happens to be involved with a man who was directly associated with the murder of two men and the theft of our state's beloved Kensington stone. The choice of this woman by my opponent for head of the State Police shows she is totally incompetent to..." Max turned off the television.

"Well, that sucks," Max said to Assumpta.

"It certainly does," Assumpta replied.

"What can we do?" Max asked.

"I think I have an idea. Do you still have the stone in your possession?" Assumpta questioned.

"Yes," Max told her, puzzled, "We have it in the storage room at the station. It's evidence in the theft."

"Great. Get it out and find some way to display it out in front of the police station," Assumpta told her.

"Why?" Max asked.

"Lars is calling the press and scheduling a press conference at the Royal Oaks Police Department in one hour. Can you be ready?" Assumpta exclaimed.

"Ready for what?" Max questioned.

"You're coming out party and by the way, bring your citation you got from Russell," Assumpta demanded.

Chapter 37

Max had everything ready by the time she saw Assumpta's limo and a catering van following behind, pull into the police station parking lot. The weather was getting colder and starting to spit snowflakes, but the press corps was patiently standing outside the building waiting for the conference to start.

Assumpta and Lars went into the building through the parking lot door and greeted Max.

"Everything ready?" she asked Max.

"Yes. We have a podium with a microphone and speakers set up and the Kensington stone is propped up on a table with a blanket over it out front," Max told her.

"Great, and you got your citation? she asked. Max handed her the rolled-up accommodation given to her by Ted Russell.

"Great. Lars has been working on my speech on the way here, so I guess we're ready to go," Assumpta said, taking a deep breath. Lars handed her a couple of sheets of paper as she went through the front door and out to the waiting press.

There were about twenty reporters along with three television stations set up and ready for Assumpta to speak.

"Greetings and thank you for coming out on such short notice," she said, moving behind the podium. "I know the weather isn't cooperating, but I'll try to get through this as quickly as possible. Oh, and bye the way, there will be coffee, hot cider, and snacks waiting for you in the building after the question session. So, the fewer questions you have, the quicker we can get inside," Assumpta opened with, pulling her coat tighter around her. This drew some laughs and applause from the cold, waiting press.

Assumpta then began her speech. "I'm sure you've seen my political rival, Ted Russell's, earlier press conference, and just to clear the record, I would like to point out a few inaccuracies and inconsistencies that Mr. Russell stated in his speech.

"In his statement this afternoon, he maligned and misrepresented my nominee for head of the Minnesota State Police. She is Chief of Police of Royal Oaks, Maxine Somers.

I haven't known Royal Oaks Police Chief Maxine Somers for very long. But in that short period, I have come to admire her ability, courage, and dedication to her job. Last year was she not only tortured and buried alive, but she was able to crawl out of her grave and bring down one of the most insidious drug gangs in this section of the state. Unfortunately, a leader of the drug gang was one of her fellow officers, who in a cowardly act of revenge, tried to ambush her on the side of a highway. Only through luck, was she able to shoot her assailant before he shot her.

In fact, she was so brave that she was given an accommodation by our esteemed State Attorney General. A fact he seems to have forgotten." Assumpta stated, then held up Max's citation for the press to see.

"On another note, you all have heard and reported on about the terrible tragedy of the deaths of two men, and the theft of the Kensington stone at the Medieval fair." She paused for a dramatic flair. "John Randall, the owner of Minneapolis business, Randall Security, and the designer of the Kensington stone exhibit, was tragically struck down while trying to foil the theft of the Kensington Stone. Two of the three assailants were unfortunately killed in the explosion during the theft."

Only through hard work and dogged diligence, was Chief Somers able to apprehend the third assailant and recover the Kensington stone," she concluded, as she walked over to the table and pulled back the snow- covered blanket, revealing the Kensington stone, displayed on the table.

The Press Corp moved forward to take pictures of Assumpta and the stone. The TV station cameras all panned in to get a better position. Finally, reporters asked Max to stand next to Assumpta and the stone. As they were posing for the press, Assumpta whispered to Max, "I never thought I'd be upstaged by a rock," Max just nodded her head and smiled.

After several minutes of picture taking, Assumpta asked if there were anymore questions. The reporters continued on asking other questions about the campaign, but finally Assumpta took the last one and asked everybody to move inside for refreshments.

Once inside, Max noticed Mayor Price standing next to the refreshment table, signaling for Max to come and talk to him. Walking over, she asked him, "What's up, boss?"

"I don't think this little party is in the police department budget, but it is really great publicity for the town. Way to go, Chief," he stated.

"Thanks, Mayor," Max replied. "It was kind of last minute."

"Next time, get permission," he told her sternly but with a smile. He then walked away, eating a chocolate chip cookie, looking for a reporter to talk to.

After twenty minutes, Assumpta broke free from the reporters and walked up to Max. Lars followed right behind her.

"Well, I think we avoided a major disaster, and this weather couldn't have come at a more perfect time," Assumpta said, smiling at Max.

"Isn't this snow bad for the election? Max asked.

"Tell her Lars," Assumpta said.

"This snow is great for us. The polls show us leading with the younger voters. Older people tend not to vote with inclement weather, while young people do. The snow couldn't come at a better time," Lars explained.

"Makes sense, I guess," Max replied. "But one thing I do want to know."

"What's that?" Assumpta questioned.

"Who was that superhero you were describing to the press, when we were outside?" she asked with a smile.

"Do you remember what I told you was the first thing a politician learns?" Assumpta asked.

"How to lie," Max responded, not sure if it was a compliment or not.

It took a while to clear out the press, clean up the mess left behind, and secure the stone back in the evidence room. Assumpta and Lars left in their limo. The caterers loaded up their belongings, and things got back to normal at the police station.

It didn't take long after the euphoric high of the press conference, for reality to bring Max back to normal. Unfortunately, it was too late for her to call Mark Richards back.

Chapter 38

With her deputy chief off work for a few days because of his new baby, Max was working the night shift until he came back.

Max got off of her shift and went home to get some rest. The first winter snow had left about six inches of wet, heavy accumulation that made driving very slick. There were several messages on her phone answering machine. One from Randall's doctor at the hospital, one from Ted Russell, and a couple of spam messages. She kept the first two and deleted the spam. She knew it was too early for her to return the doctor's or Russell's messages and vowed to call them back later in the morning.

After changing out of her uniform, she fixed some breakfast and laid down to rest for a while.

Her brain was so worked up that she found sleep impossible to achieve. Finally getting up, she decided that she might as well go and vote.

Heading to the High School gymnasium where the polling station was set up for the community, she mulled over one of the key issues on the Royal Oaks ballot. The mayor had taken her request for more supervisors in the police department and as he promised, examined the numbers. After looking at the expenditures involved, he decided to take a different direction instead.

He proposed to the city council that the whole police department be restructured. Instead of two twelve- hour shifts a day, they change the schedule to three eight-hour shifts. He told the council that even with the increase in personnel needed, in the long run they would save money on overtime pay.

The city council decided to put the item on the local ballot and let the local voters decide the issue. Max wasn't sure which way to vote, but win or lose, she knew that her police department was going to change.

Arriving at the polling place, she realized Lars was right about the voter turnout. Most of the people were younger with only a smattering of older voters turning up. After casting her vote, she returned home to make her phone calls.

The first call to Randall's doctor made her feel euphoric. He told her that they were going to start bringing John out of his coma and that he should be conscious soon. After hanging up the phone, she made the phone call to Ted Russell. She really didn't want to make the call, but she knew she would have to get it over with.

"Chief Somers, I need to talk to you today. Meet me at my campaign headquarters on Marquette Avenue before five o'clock today," he commanded, sounding very upset and irritated. "Make sure you're wearing your police uniform or after today I'll make sure you'll be wearing a prison uniform, understand?"

Max was taken aback by the tone of his voice. She responded, "Yes sir, I understand. Can I ask what this is concerning, sir?" Max asked.

"Never mind what it's about, just be there," he repeated angerly.

"Yes sir," Max replied.

Max hung up the phone both relieved it was over, and yet dreading the future meeting in the afternoon. She then proceeded to call Mark Richard and give him the good news about Randall's improvement.

"That's fantastic news," he told Max. She seemed to hear some trepidation in his voice.

"Any more news on Jack Taylor's finances?" She asked.

"Funny you should ask," Mark replied, "It seems that ninety per cent of his income seems to be coming from deposits in Cancun banks. We know where that money was coming from. The other ten percent is accounted for from legitimate services, in and around Bemidji. But it's his withdrawals that are puzzling me. He's making deposits of ten thousand dollars every month into a bank account located in downtown Minneapolis."

"Who owns the account?" Max questioned.

"I can't tell. The account is registered to a dummy corporation, which in turn is registered to another dummy corporation. I'm having difficulty locating the name of who owns the accounts," Mark explained.

"Any idea?" Max asked.

"My best guess is either Taylor is using these companies as tax shelters for himself or he's making payments to someone. It could be possible he is being blackmailed," Mark responded,

"What can you do to find out?" Max replied, her curiosity aroused,

"I need to call some of Randall's friends in Washington. Maybe they can be of some help," Mark told her.

"How long will that take?" she asked again.

"They are going to need to get a warrant to get into those accounts. They really can't do anything without it. That should take an hour or two, depending on if they can find a friendly judge. With a warrant, it should only take two or three hours to do a forensic tracking of those accounts. So, I guess we would know something early this afternoon." Mark explained.

"Sounds good," Max responded, "by the way, how did you get all of the other information for me?"

Mark was silent for a few seconds, then told her, "I hacked the accounts, but you never heard that from me."

"So, all this other information would be inadmissible in court?" she questioned.

Silence again, then he replied, "Yes, but I promise you, I'll get the necessary paperwork needed with a proper warrant and send it to you."

"Good, I don't want anybody to escape justice because of a technicality, like no warrant," She told Mark.

"Don't worry. I'll cover all the bases," He responded.

Max then tried to get ahold of Assumpta. She got Lars instead.

"Good morning, Chief," Lars stated. "My sister is giving a speech right now and isn't available. Anything I can do?"

Max informed him of the phone conversation she had with Ted Russell, earlier. After she finished, she waited for his reply. She heard only silence on the other end of the phone.

"Hello? Lars, are your there?" Max asked.

After a short pause, he responded. "Yah, I'm still here. Listen, let me talk with my sister after she's done giving her speech. I'll give you a call back. Okay?"

"Okay, fine. Let me know what your thoughts are, as soon as possible," Max replied.

"Will do. She's just finishing up now. I'll get back to you within the hour," he explained,

"Thanks, Lars," Max told him as she hung up the phone.

Chapter 39

The rest of the morning passed slowly for Max, as she waited for her phone calls from Mark and Assumpta. The call from Assumpta came first.

"Tell me exactly what Turner said to you," Assumpta asked. Max proceeded to repeat the gist of the conversation she had with the State District Attorney and stressed the unpleasant tone in his voice.

"Go to the meeting with him," Assumpta told her. "My sources tell me that he is preparing for a last-minute press conference. My guess is that he is going to force you to make some kind of statement that he hopes will sway the election. Whatever it is, we have no idea. Just go along with it as best you can."

"How's the election going?" Max questioned, trying to change the subject.

"Exit surveys of the voters show we started strong, but Turner has been bussing nursing home and senior citizens into the voting stations in such quantities, that at this time, it appears to be a dead heat. Lars thinks that he's going to use you and the press for a last-minute surge on the six o'clock news, to try and push him over the top with the voters," Assumpta told her.

"Why don't you be there too? Maybe hijack the press conference, and steal some of his thunder?" Max suggested.

Max could hear Assumpta telling Lars what she had just suggested. Then Assumpta responded to Max. "Lars says that you have a great idea, and that we'll definitely do it. You're really getting a handle on this politicking game, girlfriend."

"Glad I could help. So, I'll see you later in Minneapolis?" Max asked.

"We'll be there. Just stay calm and we'll get through this. Okay?" Assumpta assured.

"Okay, and thanks." Max told her'

"No problem. I'll see you later this afternoon," Assumpta reassured her.

After hanging up, she started feeling better, but remembered she didn't tell Assumpta about the good news concerning Randall. She thought about calling her back but decided not to.

It wasn't until a couple of hours later that Mark called back.

"Find anything?" She asked him.

"Yes." He replied. Actually, quite a bit."

"Good news?" Max asked again.

"Maybe, you tell me. First of all, guess who represented Jack Taylor in a drug possession case twelve years ago, and guess who represented Newgate, Sorenson and Nash in a hit and run case fifteen years ago?

"No idea. Who?" Max questioned.

"Wait, hold on. Guess how Taylor got off in his trial?" Again, he asked her, continuing, "It couldn't be proved, but the rumor was that there was likely a bribed juror. And in the Newgate, Sorenson and Nash trial, they were found not guilty when a surprise witness came forward at the last second and testified that they were over fifty miles away from the accident when it happened, essentially giving them an iron clad alibi," Mark told her excitedly.

"And last but not least, guess who owns the bank account that Jack Taylor was sending ten thousand dollars to every month as campaign donations?" Mark finished.

"Ted Russell?" She said incredulously, the truth dawning on her, "State District Attorney, Ted Russell?"

"One and the same. But the bad news is that it still doesn't prove that he was involved in the explosion and theft at the medieval fair," Mark added.

"No, it doesn't, but it sure is a smoking gun, isn't it?" she stated. "But it is a coincidence, and I don't believe in coincidences. I don't know if Taylor knew who was blackmailing him, but I'm pretty sure that Nash isn't telling all that he knows. He rolled over and confessed way too fast. Maybe he thinks he has protection?"

"Like a State District Attorney?" Mark questioned.

"Maybe, I think I'm going to have a few more words with him and find out what else he knows that he's not telling us." she told him.

"Good luck. If you need anything else, just let me know," he responded.

"Oh, by the way, Randall's doctor informed me they are bringing him out of the coma. He should be conscious tomorrow or the next day," Max exclaimed.

"Fantastic news. It will be good to see him up and around soon." Mark responded. This time there was definitely a strange sound in his voice.

Max sat down on her couch for a few minutes and digested all of the information she had just been given. Finally, she got up and grabbed her service revolver, along with her ID, and headed out to her car. Driving to the police station, she planned her strategy needed to get the information she wanted.

Arriving at the station in street clothes, she was greeted by some raised eyebrows of approval from a couple of officers that were not on patrol. Officer Jenkins merely shook his head in acknowledgement. Max asked him to bring Nash out of the holding cell and move him to the interrogation room. While waiting in the room, she started implementing her plan by again making up a dummy file folder with a bunch of empty sheets of paper in it.

After about ten minutes, Officer Jenkins brought Nash into the room. She told him to handcuff Nash to the rail bolted down on the table. After he was secured, she asked Jenkins to wait outside the door. After Jenkins left the room, she sat back and stared at the prisoner. After a couple of minutes of silence between the two, Nash final broke the silence by asking, "What?"

Max just smiled at him, then stated, "Well Mr. Nash, you haven't been exactly honest with me, have you?"

"What do you mean?" he asked.

"I've been looking over your record. You've had some very interesting brushes with the law, haven't you?" she told him, as she tapped her finger on the file folder.

"Never been convicted," Nash told her.

"No, never been convicted. Guess that was because you had a really good lawyer. You did have a really good lawyer, didn't you, Mr. Nash?" as she tapped on the manilla folder on the table again. Max saw his eyes scrutinize the file folder she was tapping. She thought he turned several shades of white.

"Maybe? Why?" he questioned.

"Well, I think we need to take another look at that old hit and run incident from a few years ago. What was there, two fatalities? An older, retired man and his wife. if the record is correct," she told him, still tapping on the file folder.

"I was already tried for that. The jury found me innocent, and you can't try me again, you know, double jeopardy," he expounded.

"Very good, Mr. Nash. Your attorney has advised you accurately, but what he didn't tell you that you can be retried if there is evidence of malfeasance during the trial." Max told him.

"What? What is this malfeasance thing you're talking about?" he asked her, now visibly shaken.

"Malfeasance means that someone didn't do their job properly or lied or provided false evidence in a trial," she explained. "You wouldn't know if any of those things happened during your trial, do you?" she said, still tapping her finger on the file folder.

Nash sat like a stone as he contemplated his options. Finally, he asked her, "What can you do for me? I'll tell you what you want to know, but I need some kind of deal."

Max felt a wave of relief, realizing that her ploy had worked. Thinking over her options, she told him, "Look, I'm not out to crucify you for your old hit and run. But there's not much I can do about your possession of stolen property and breaking and entering. although I can help you with felony assault and manslaughter.

"With any luck you'll get five to ten and be out in a couple with good behavior," she explained to him. "Who I really want is your lawyer."

Nash dejectedly sat back in his chair and mulled over his next move.

"Okay, what do you want?" he stated.

Max reached over and turned on the recorder and took out her cell phone and turned on the video application. She then went to the door and asked the waiting Officer Jenkins to come in.

"Mr. Nash would like to make a statement," she told him. Jenkins came in and sat on the chair next to Max.

"Okay Mr. Nash, start at the beginning," she instructed.

Nash started his narrative by explaining that he had been approached by his old lawyer, Ted Russell about doing a job for him. At the beginning Nash wasn't interested, but Russell turned on the pressure by explaining how he was owed because he 'found' a witness to cover for him and his two associates in the hit and run case, even though they all knew the witness was lying.

Nash told Max that Russell used Jack Turner to give him and his two buddies each ten thousand dollars to steal the stone for him. He said that Russell had a vehicle ready for them at an airport in Bemidji and all they had to do was go and get it and return it when the job was done.

Russell told them that they were to scout the exhibit the day before the heist, which was easy since they were all members of the SVR. He told them where the cameras were located but he didn't know where the proximity alarm was.

Russell had informed the trio, that when they made a signal, he would have the cameras turned off remotely since he had hacked into the alarm system. He also told us that we should be prepared for an intruder that he would lure onto the site, so as to put the blame of the theft on him.

Max now knew why Randall was at the exhibit that night. He had been lured there by Ted Russell, after hacking Assumpta's phone.

Nash continued, saying they were to blow the exhibit, load up the stone and get out of there, but what Russell didn't count on was the three of them deciding to have a few drinks at a bar beforehand. By the time we got to the fair, they had a few too many and were pretty loaded.

Nash told her that just when Ron and Stan lit the fuses to blow the exhibit, the intruder appeared and confronted them. They were scared by him so much, he assumed they forgot to take cover and were killed in the explosion. He said that upon hearing the explosion, he ran into the longhouse through the blown-out hole in the wall and saw the three men who appeared to be dead. He proceeded to load up the stone, struggling to do so, and drove out of the emergency gate, scraping the side pole on his way out.

Nash went on to explain that he was to text Russell the location of the stone once he had deposited it in a safe place and returned the Hummer.

After Nash had told Max his narrative, she had to ask him, "Why? Why did Russell need the Kensington stone so badly?"

"The election. He was going to miraculously recover it and make it appear he was the big hero to the press. He knew he was in for a fight for his political life, so he was going to bolster his ratings by finding the stone at the last minute, but instead, you beat him to it. So now he has no big surprise," Nash explained to her.

Max realized that with Russell's big surprise ruined, that she would now become his new big surprise. She was determined not to let that happen. She knew that with such a tight political race, Russell's plan just might work unless she could throw a wrench into it.

Sending Mr. Nash back to his cell, she realized what her next steps would be. She grabbed the video tape out of the recorder from the interrogation room and headed over to the mayor's office. Arriving at his office, she asked him to view the video of the interrogation of Nash. After the video was over, the mayor sat back in his chair, and let out a big sigh.

"You got the old bastard," he exclaimed. "It's about time."

"What can we do with it?" Max questioned. She then explained to him Russell's demand for her to meet him at his campaign headquarters at five o'clock that afternoon and hypothesized what he had in store for her.

"The hell he will," he said. "Can I borrow the tape? Do you have a backup copy?" he asked.

"On my phone," she told him.

"Perfect," he exclaimed. "Make another copy and stash it somewhere safe. Keep your phone on and with you. I'm going to show it to a couple of my associates and then I'll call you and tell you what to do. Got it?" he instructed.

"What's the plan?" she questioned.

"The less you know, the better you'll be. Just trust me and go meet with Russell. You'll get my phone call with instructions. Okay?" he told her, placing the video tape in a manilla envelope. Leaving the mayor's office, Max felt a combination of hope and dread. Fear of meeting with Russell and hope that the ordeal would soon be over.

Later in the day, Max left Royal Oaks for her meeting with Russell. The drive into Minneapolis was the longest one she had ever made. Arriving at the downtown area of the meeting, Max parked her car in a parking lot and took a covered walkway to the hotel for the appointed meeting. Russell had booked a conference room in the hotel where his campaign headquarters was located.

Arriving earlier than Russell had demanded, she saw Lars standing by the walkway opening of the hotel, waiting for her. Spotting her, he quickly walked over and ushered her into the lobby of the hotel. Assumpta was waiting in the corner of the lobby wearing the black suit she had worn the first day that Max had met her at the Medieval fair. She also wore a black wide brimmed hat, with a veil over her face to help disguise her, in case any passerby might possibly identify her.

"Good, you're here. I was almost afraid you wouldn't come," Assumpta told her.

"Wouldn't miss it for the world," Max replied sarcastically.

"Here's what to expect when we go upstairs to Russell's watch party. There will be a lot of people, a mix of his supporters and press. He probably will have some law officers present as security. There almost certainly will be a stage or podium from where he plans to make his victory speech along with a lot of big screen TVs scattered throughout the room. There will be noise and confusion from the crowd as the exit polls and projections are announced," Assumpta informed her. "Voting doesn't close until seven o'clock, so his big surprise involving you has to take place at five in order for the news channels to get it on the five- thirty news," Assumpta finished.

"Okay, I guess I'm ready," Max assured them. "Let's get this over with."

Assumpta nodded her head in agreement, then told Lars, "Give it to her."

Lars took an envelope from his inside breast pocket of his suit jacket and handed it to Max.

"Open it after this is all over," she instructed Max.

Max took the envelope, looked curiously at it, folded it, and placed it in her back pants pocket. "Let's go," she told them, as she headed for the elevator.

Chapter 40

The elevator ride up one floor seemed an eternity to Max. As the elevator doors opened, she paused getting off. Assumpta took her hand and gave it a reassuring squeeze. Stepping off the elevator and walking up to the conference room door, she took a deep breath and walked in.

The scene that Assumpta had described was exactly as she said it would be. Nobody paid any attention to her as she entered the room, figuring that with her uniform on, she was just one of the security people. She started heading toward the stage and podium located at the front of the room. The conference room was crowded and noisy. Making it about halfway through the crowd, she suddenly felt her cell phone vibrating in her pocket.

Answering it, she was ecstatic to see two text messages from the mayor. The first text read,

"All is ready. Arrest him. See following text. Mayor Price," Pulling up the second text, it said,

"Any problems, show him the attachment." Max pulled up the attachment on her phone. It was a copy of an arrest warrant for Ted Russell, signed by a federal district judge, whom she didn't know.

How the Hell did Mayor Price pull that off? she thought to herself. Looking behind her, through the crowd, to locate Assumpta and Lars, she realized they were nowhere in sight. She was all alone.

Steeling her courage, she made her way through the crowd and up to the stage. Ted Russell was standing there, flanked by several other people and two police officers beside him.

As she approached the stage, Russell spotted her and gestured for her to join him. Locating a set of stairs, Max made her way up to the stage and walked over to him. Just as she approached him, someone turned up the PA systems to amplify the sound from the huge TVs mounted on the walls around the room. The news bulletin said, "... and the exit polls for the race for State District Attorney shows it's a very small lead for newcomer, Assumpta Morgan, over incumbent Ted Russell. We're not prepared to make any projections as all votes are not in yet with still over two hours to go before the polls close. In other races the polls are showing the Governor's race to be...." A loud groan came from the crowd as the sound was turned back down.

As Max drew closer to Russell, he moved to her, grabbed her arm forcefully, and quickly led her off to the side of the stage. "Good, you're here, and just in time. Now listen to me, and listen to me good, lady. You're going to go up to the microphone and announce to everybody in the room here, that I was instrumental in the recovery of the Kensington stone. Got it?" he threatened, then continuing. "And if you don't, my next announcement will be your arrest for the murder of Tad Paulson. Do you understand me?"

"But I've been cleared of that charge, Sir," Max countered.

"Do you think those idiots out there in this crowd care? Do you think the stupid press cares? Do you think those sheep called voters care? All the press wants is something sensational to put on the air. True or not, they don't give a damn. In a couple of days, it will just be old news, and nobody will pay a damn bit of attention to it.

"So, you just get up to the microphone and make your announcement and then you can go home to your little rat hole, arrest drunks, and live your life in mediocrity. Now go over there and do it," he threatened.

Pointing at one of his assistants on the stage to come over, they both waited for him to walk over to join them. "Jack, this is Police Chief Maxine Somers from Royal Oaks, and she has a very important announcement to make to the people here. Go and quiet them down and then introduce her. And make it quick," he ordered him.

The dutiful assistant promptly followed his orders and using the microphone, got the attention of the room. When all was quiet, he announced, "Ladies and gentlemen and members of the press, I'd like to introduce Police Chief Maxine Somers from the town of Royal Oaks, Minnesota. She has a very important announcement to make.

Max walked slowly up to the microphone on the podium. The assistant moved away from the podium and suddenly she felt very, very alone in the room full of people with their eyes all on her. Wetting her lips, she began, "I think everybody here knows that the Medieval fair outside of Royal Oaks has had a terrible tragedy with the theft of the Kensington stone, and the injury of one person, and the death of two other individuals involved. Thankfully, the stone has been safely recovered, and several individuals apprehended in the theft." Looking over at Russell, she saw the broad, infuriating grin on his face.

"However, one individual, the mastermind of the theft, has not been apprehended yet. I am here to rectify that problem," Looking again at Russell, she saw the grin was gone from his countenance. "I am here to arrest Mr. Ted Russell for the crime of felony theft, bribery, extortion, and money laundering." The whole room erupted into chaos with some people shouting and the press eagerly pushing forward to take photos. Russell ran over to the microphone, pushing Max out of the way, and yelling into the microphone, "This is all a lie. A lie fabricated by my opponent to discredit me. Don't fall for it. It's all a lie." Then turning to the police officers on the stage, he yelled, "Officers, arrest this woman and get her out of here."

The two police deputies looked at each other, one of them got out a pair of handcuffs and started walking toward Max. She fumbled for the cell phone in her pants pocket and started to pull up the copy of the arrest warrant on her phone, getting ready to show them the warrant.

The two officers instead walked past her and to her astonishment, placed the handcuffs on Russell. Ted Russell now stood on the stage, his hands secured in front of him, fully in shock.

The shock quickly wore off as a multitude of camera flashes from the press seemed to go off in unison, and the room erupted in confusion.

"What? What are you doing? Arrest her," he screamed, pointing at Max.

"Can't, Sir. We got our orders," the first officer stated.

"From whom?" Russell yelled in a rage, turning red in the face.

"The Governor," the second officer explained.

The reality of his situation quickly set in. Before anyone could react, Russell lunged at the second officer and grabbed the gun out of his holster. Using it to keep the two officers at bay, he then pointed it at Max. "You're going to die, bitch!" he screamed at the top of his lungs.

The whole conference center went suddenly silent, watching what would happen next.

After what seemed like an eternity but was in reality only seconds, Max closed her eyes, and prepared to die.

A shot rang out. Max flinched, awaiting the pain she knew was coming, and then, nothing.

Opening her eyes, she saw, as if in slow motion, the whole room trying to duck for cover. Then looking at Russell, she saw him slowly falling to the floor, a red stain growing on his shoulder, and quickly looking back to the floor of the convention, she saw a lone man standing among all the cowering people, pointing his gun at Russell. It was Mr. Smith, Assumpta's old security guard. The same Mr. Smith she had met so long ago in the long house in the Viking village.

The two police officers quickly jumped into action. The one officer who had his weapon taken by Russell, ran over to him and retrieved the weapon from where it had fallen on the floor. He then checked Russell out and got on his portable radio and called for backup and an ambulance.

The second officer, with his gun drawn quickly but cautiously, went onto the convention floor and approached Mr. Smith. Mr. Smith stood there silently with his empty hands in the air waiting for the approaching officer. The rest of the people, except for the press, were making a hasty retreat out of the convention room. Max just stood still on the stage, slowly realizing the reality of her situation.

Finally, her instincts kicked in and she went over to the officer attending Russell.

"Is he alright?" she questioned.

"Yeah, he'll recover. The guy that shot him knew what he was doing, or Russell was very lucky. The bullet went in the exact right spot to disarm but not kill," the officer told her.

About the same time, the second officer had brought Mr. Smith with handcuffs on, up the stage.

"You alright, Chief Somers?" Smith asked her.

"Yeah, just fine. Thanks to you. Mr. Smith," she replied, thankfully.

"You know him?" the second officer questioned.

"Yes, and if my instincts are correct, you'll probably find a shield on him," Max stated, in a matter-of-fact tone of voice.

Smith just smiled at her and told the officer, "Right inside shoulder pocket."

The officer searched the pocket and retrieved a flat leather wallet. Opening it up revealed a gold badge. The officer looked it over and then took the handcuffs off of him and returned his wallet to him.

"Sorry, Agent Smith," the officer told him, apologetically, giving him back his service revolver.

"No problem," Smith replied. Then turning to the other officer, told him, "Now you know why you were taught in training to handcuff a suspect's hands behind the back of the body. That way you'll lose your weapon a lot less."

The offending officer turned red from embarrassment and replied, "Thank you, Sir. I'll remember it."

By this time, the press was having a field day taking pictures of the scene. Even a couple of reporters from the local TV stations were setting up television cameras and demanding interviews. The requested police backup and the ambulance personnel finally arrived, transferring the wounded Russell off to the hospital. The two officers accompanied the ambulance so they could fill out their reports.

Finally, after the reporters had all left, only Max and Smith remained in the cavernous, empty conference room. Nobody had bothered to turn off the big screen televisions. On the way out of the hall, she looked up at the screens and observed the news break, reporting the shooting and arrest of State Attorney General Ted Russell.

I wonder if Assumpta dreamt about winning the vote, this way? she thought to herself.

Walking out of the hotel on their way to the parking garage, she stopped on the overhead walkway and asked Mr. Smith, "So tell me the truth. Who are you?"

Smith just smiled and said, "I'm your best friend. John brought me in from the Houston office after your little escapade last year. He was concerned that there might still be some people out there who still want revenge on you, so I was assigned as a protective agent to keep you safe at all times."

"You've been following me ever since last year?" Max asked.

"Me or one of my associates. We had to escalate our coverage after John was injured." He replied.

"But why the charade of working for Assumpta?" she questioned.

"It was a ploy to check her off the list of possible revenge suspects." he stated.

"How could she be wanting revenge on me? I didn't even know her until I met you, along with her, at the Medieval fair," Max questioned.

"True, but as part of our surveillance, we keep a tab on any unusual inquiries about you on the internet and treat them as a possible threat," he told her.

"She did inquiries about me on the internet?" Max asked.

"A lot of them. It wasn't until we figured out what her job intentions were for you, that I stopped working for her," he explained.

Satisfied with his answers, she had only one last question for him. "What agency do you work for?" she asked him.

He just smiled at her and replied, "The same one John works for." He then turned and walked the other way, down the covered walkway and into the darkness of the Minnesota evening.

Chapter 41

Arriving back at her apartment, Max was so tired and exhausted, all she had strength for was getting into bed. She observed that her answering machine had a couple of dozen messages on it, but she resolved to not answer and ignore them until the next morning.

Undressing, she spotted the envelope in her back pants pocket, the one that Assumpta had given her in the hotel lobby. Placing it on the night stand next to her bed, she made herself a promise that she would read it first thing in the morning.

She laid down in her bed, determined to fall asleep, but all she could think about was the unread letter. Finally, after tossing and turning for twenty minutes, she finally turned on the lamp by her nightstand and opened the letter sitting there. It read,

"Max- I must tell you how much I admire and respect you. Not only that but I feel you're like a sister to me. A sister I never had.

I want you to know something important. I dream about you. You've been in my dreams now for over a year. I dreamt about you long before I met you. When I did meet you and John that first time at the Viking village, I knew you immediately, and I knew you were the right person that I wanted for my friend, and also for the head of the State Police.

I knew you would accept my job offer before you did. It was in my dreams. But recently you have been absent from them. That absence has convinced me that although you have accepted my offer, you will never take the job.

You won't be seeing me for a while, but eventually you will see me again. How do I know this? I've seen it in my dreams. Remember, you and I share the sightline, and we'll always be in each other's dreams. I'm always here for you. Assumpta."

Max finally fell asleep much later, trying to figure out the meaning of Assumpta's cryptic letter.

Epilogue

Max awoke the next morning feeling as tired as she did the night before. The letter from Assumpta weighed heavy on her mind. Dressing in jeans and a sweatshirt, she threw on a heavy jacket to protect her from the Minnesota, November cold.

Today was the day she would finally get to see John awake at the hospital, after more than two months in a drug- induced coma. His body had healed and the swelling in his head had gone down, and he was going to live.

Max had made a promise to herself that she was going to be present when he woke up, so she left early for the hospital. Arriving at the hospital, she quickly went to the third floor and headed down the hall to Randall's room.

Arriving at his door, she noticed the white board next to it, had been cleaned off. Opening the door, she saw that his bed was empty, stripped of the blankets, sheets, and pillow. She thought that maybe they had moved him to a different room now that he was so much improved.

Going to the nurse's station, she asked where John Randall's new room was.

The nurse on duty got on the computer to find his new room. After checking the screen, she revealed to her, "He'd was checked out of the hospital during the night."

"What do you mean, checked out?" Max replied, almost hysterical.

"Look, let me get his doctor. He can explain," the nurse told her, trying to calm her down.

It took ten minutes after the page for the doctor, before he showed up. Max saw him walking down the hallway towards the nurse's station. When he finally got there, Max demanded to know where Randall was.

"He was checked out last night by his family. His sister had an ambulance service, several attendants, and all the proper paperwork to transfer him to a different facility," the Doctor informed Max.

What do you mean, his sister?" Max demanded.

"Tall, good looking, older woman," he said, looking at the computer screen. "Here it is," pointing to the computer screen. "The name she gave is Hutchins, Ann Hutchins."

"I don't know who checked him out, because my John Randall doesn't have any brothers or sisters. He's an only child," Max exclaimed.

Don't miss out!

Visit the website below and you can sign up to receive emails whenever T.M. Erwin publishes a new book. There's no charge and no obligation.

https://books2read.com/r/B-A-IUWL-XCOVB

BOOKS2READ

Connecting independent readers to independent writers.

Did you love *Sightline*? Then you should read *Frostline*[1] by T.M. Erwin!

[2]

Maxine Somers is a L.A. beat cop that finds herself working as a small town detective just outside Minneapolis, Minnesota. She finds her idyllic job anything peaceful with having to deal with drug traffickers, murders and a new boyfriend .Her investigations takes her from Minnesota all the way to southern Texas and back again, to try and solve her case.

---

1. https://books2read.com/u/mKzkJ9

2. https://books2read.com/u/mKzkJ9

www.ingramcontent.com/pod-product-compliance
Lightning Source LLC
Chambersburg PA
CBHW050508160726
48003CB00001B/209